DYBBUK

A NOVELLA

JOHN BALTISBERGER

IN THE DOORWAY

For Naturre, Z''l

SATURDAY

The woman sat alone in the small room, her eyes red and puffy from sobbing. Sorrow had nearly consumed her, but grief was secondary now. Now, her primary emotion was rage. She felt rage for many things, her situation, the circumstances life had thrust on her, for all the loss she had been forced to endure while pretending her feelings were unbecoming. Stoicism in the face of sadness, and anger she felt could wash away all of creation.

But most of all, she raged against the world and the men who ruled over it.

There were always stories of powerful women who bucked against the authority of men, against the circumstances, situations, and stations that were given to them. Some of them were more modern heroes of feminism. Some of them were old. Older than the city, older than even their people and their laws. So old that to invoke them was to call upon the bones of the world. She needed that now.

She needed the world to groan in pain with her. She needed the earth to shake with her fury. She needed the old stories to protect—no, not protect, punish. She no longer cared about safety or morality, for what use were either in a world that sought to hold her down and give her nothing?

Before her sat a small cigar box. She had placed within it things that seemed appropriate. From all of her secretive research—done in furtive hunts across many months—she knew only a few items were actually necessary. The research had been done for fun at first, but as she got older and wiser, she knew it was for a purpose. It was not for childish things but for power. The power to finally take her place in the world, a place she felt she deserved. But now, now she only wanted the power to make them pay.

She poured the jar of teeth into the box. They had come from children who placed them under their pillows, from the trashcan of a local dentist who did not follow protocol, and, when all else failed, from clandestine trips to the graveyard, stolen from the mouths of those who no longer needed them. She set the empty jar aside.

One more thing, one more component. She grabbed the pliers and lifted them to her mouth. Opening as wide as she could, she gripped her upper left molar. She was scared of the pain. But her sorrow made her numb to it, her anger gave her the strength. She wrenched, twisting and pulling, dragging the tooth out with all of her might. Blood poured from the wound, pooling in her mouth. She spat a wad of it into the box and added her tooth to the pile.

Quickly, she grabbed a candle and began sealing the box with wax, spitting mouthfuls of blood into the now empty tooth jar whenever it threatened to choke her. After several minutes in the near dark, she grabbed a small knife and carved a single word into the box—no, not a word, a name.

לִילִית

MONDAY

1

Being back in New York made Eli's skin crawl. The old brick buildings, the stagnant air, and the bustle of people like maggots swarming over the rotting carcass of the American dream. Every aspect sickened him. It was one of the reasons he had gone into tech—generally, it confined him to working in hubs of progress, pushing into the future in cities like Los Angeles, San Fransisco, or Austin. It let him avoid places mired in history, dedicated to the past and lineage.

He had left this cesspit of a city when he was 16, abandoning home, community, family, and the past they all clung to so fiercely. He had been an explorer then, fleeing ever westward towards a new mecca that offered salvation from everything he had grown to despise. But, of course, with the pandemic waning, everyone was jumping at the opportunity to hold live events. Conventions, symposiums, in-person demos, and, worst of all, trade shows. Any excuse at all to get out of the house and see people in the flesh was jumped at.

Not Eli. He had been happy in his hole, isolated from the

world except for his cat and his girlfriend. Even gearing up for Christmas was a digital affair. They had a fake tree, fake snow, even fake frost for the balmy 80-degree California winter. But here he was, with real snow and real frost in the very cold streets of New York City. A winter wonderland of muddy slush and shitty people all milling about in the streets like aimless chickens.

The trade show itself had been an exercise in futility. Eli had gone on to explain the technical aspects of their solution to rooms full of vendors and potential clients. But the truth was these CIOs and CISOs didn't care; they didn't come to buy their infrastructure services. Even if they had, they wouldn't care about the technical aspects; they just wanted to know what to expect as end users. They came specifically to visit whores and strippers in a new city while sipping liquor that made them feel successful far from the eyes of their spouses and friends who would judge them. So Eli did his spiel and then left to return to his hotel room while sales attempted to seal the deal. Three days of this hell.

Now, all that shit was over, and Eli caught an uber to the airport, checked in, and pushed past the crowds of other idiots who tried to travel during the holiday season. At least these idiots, like him, were trying to flee this rat-infested pit of despair and pain. Eli sat down in his terminal and looked around a moment, taking in the sheer immensity of humanity around him. They reminded him of parasites jostling for position on the ass of some beast, each vying for their own bellyful of blood. He shuddered, disgusted by his own mental image, and pulled out his phone to distract himself until it was time to board.

The same constant stream of unmitigated doom and gloom assaulted him through the tiny screen of his phone. He flipped through the social networks, scrolling through all of the accounts he felt he had to follow because of his work. But it was mindless; it was rehashing and aggregation that, in the end, meant nothing—nothing to the people reposting and nothing to him. He closed out the social networks and flipped through his apps, looking for the *Nightly Disease* mobile game he had been using to kill time. It was a stupid game, managing a hotel and trying to collect owl tokens. But it required no mental effort on his part so was perfect.

He had just finished finding the last owl token in the basement when his peace was shattered by a phone call. He didn't know the number, but he recognized the area code: 718, Williamsburg. Home. He considered hitting the red button, shuffing it off to voicemail where he could deal with it later. But when was later? There was always a chance the call was from a client trying to get some last-minute tech questions answered. Or maybe one of the sales guys got locked out of his laptop and needed to show something off. They were small possibilities, but they were possibilities that could cost him his job. Frustrated by the incoming call, Eli considered whether or not he actually wanted to keep his job. Was living inside so great? You could dumpster dive outside of nice restaurants. Income was overrated. But, of course, that wasn't true. Eli was addicted to his electronics, to bacon cheeseburgers delivered to his door, and, of course, being able to afford nice things for Cynthia. And all of those things required not just an income but a pretty solid one too.

With a tired sigh that he somewhat hoped whoever calling him could hear and deduce how inconvenient they were being, he swiped the green circle to the left and brought the phone to his ear.

"Yeah?" he grunted, not meaning to sound so dismissive but not being able to help it.

"Allo, is this Elija Rosenbaum?" The voice on the other end was familiar. Not personally, but the accent was. It was that odd mix of American and forced Polish. The Yiddishized English that seemed to scrape across his skull and leave the worst scratches and scars. Eli dropped his hand from his ear, holding the phone away from him as though it were some stinging insect. He wanted to throw it, or at least hang up. But he had answered; against his better judgment, he had answered and been punished by a voice from his past that he had managed to avoid for ten years.

He could hear it still, a whisper from the other end. He hated that voice, he hated whoever it belonged to, he hated everything it represented. Eli swallowed his repulsion and, with what seemed like a monumental effort, pulled the phone back to his ear. "Uh, yeah. This is Eli," he answered.

"Elijah ..." It almost sounded like the man on the other end was correcting him, trying to get him to learn his own name. Eli could feel the rage in the form of a blinding migraine cresting the horizon and heading for him. "Elijah, you need to come home."

Eli actually laughed at that, anger dissipating in the absurdity of the statement. It was a good laugh. After ten fucking years, they expected to call in the lost sheep? Fat chance. "Look, I don't know what my family told you, but I don't think that's going to happen. I'm sorry you wasted your time tracking me down, but—"

"Elijah," the voice cut him off. "Your brother is dead."

The rest of the conversation had been a blur. Eli couldn't remember much other than numbly protesting that he had to get on a flight, that he couldn't possibly come to Brooklyn. That even if he could, his family wouldn't want him there. Eli didn't remember all of the lies or excuses he had given the man on the phone, none of them mattered, because after he hung up, Eli walked to the customer service desk and canceled his flight. It would have been easy to simply ignore the call, head back to

Cali, and celebrate Christmas by exchanging some dumb gifts, having some decent sex, and then hopping on to the computer to play games until he fell asleep. His own little Christmas tradition.

Instead, he was in an uber, watching the city slowly pass by as they drove through slush and traffic to get to a place he had no desire to go, a place he hadn't called home even when he lived there. A lot of people idolize New York City, talk about the history and the old buildings. They romanticize about the gumption of immigrants and the pursuit of the American dream while ignoring the painful truth of the past. It was violent and exploitative, and every man who walked out of the Bronx and made it big or became independently wealthy did so on the broken and battered corpses of those who failed. Then there were the communities that didn't even attempt the fantasy of success. They hunkered down, trying to keep the old world alive while desperately trying to cling to an idea of holiness that had been outdated long before they even came here.

Those were the people Eli had fled. As the uber drove into his old neighborhood, he could see the signs of their occupation. Like an infestation, they corrupted the world, stagnating change and progress. He saw them in their black coats and hats, their tallit katan's little fringes poking out like the tendrils of ghastly little jellyfish from under their shirts. The pretended humility coupled with the smug superiority of being more holy or more learned than the people they walked past. Despite Eli's best attempts to scrub his mind of the memories of this place, he couldn't help but identify the buildings and places of his childhood. There was the old Shul, looking like it was in better shape now than it ever had been in the past. And there was the yeshiva he himself had been forced to attend, tucked into a tenet housing—it didn't look better; it just looked older.

It was like leaving behind the real world and entering some twisted parody of history as told by one specific sect of Jews. Eli couldn't stomach it. He considered telling the driver to turn around and head back into civilization, but they were already coming to a stop. There it was, the apartment building his family had called home for generations now. Eli sat transfixed for a long moment, unsure if he would be able to get out of the car. His heart was constricted, held in the vise of tightening chest muscles.

"You okay, dude?" the driver asked, turning to look at Eli.

Eli glanced up and nodded. Years of pretending at normalcy and being a well-adjusted man took over, forcing him to offer a wry smile as he pushed himself out of the back of the car. "Yup. Thanks. Just having to deal with some … family stuff. You know how it is." He gave a last wave and closed the door before turning to look at the doorway.

It was a dilapidated shithole. The only difference between what it was now and what it was when he left was that more paint had peeled, more brick was visible. But everything else was the same, the same smells, people, and store fronts. Eli tried to pull some nostalgia from deep inside, some fond memories that would make him remember this place happily.

He hadn't had a completely miserable childhood. There had been good days, good friends, good times. But all of it was overshadowed by the oppressive nature of fundamentalism. Once you were free of it, everything was tinged by it. Each and every positive memory tainted by the worry it was all just conditioning and brainwashing. Eli approached the door and paused on the threshold, staring at the old, stained mezuzah. Even now, after years of neglect, his muscle memory struggled to drag his fingers to his lips. To kiss his hand and then touch the scroll imprisoned in the bit of wood there. A ritual that had been baked into his DNA. He ignored the impulse and instead rapped his knuckles against the peeling wood of the door.

Almost immediately, the door swung inward, revealing the face of an old Chassid. The man's skin drooped under the weight of age, his beard and sidelocks silverish gray. He smelled like Gołąbki and sweat. It took real effort not to recoil from the man, but Eli stood his ground, stoic in the face of the abominable. For some reason, Eli had always been repulsed by the old. They looked sick and unnatural to him. They represented the past he hated so much, the stodgy clinging to tradition and history that bored through Eli's gut like hookworms.

"Can I help you?" the man asked, his voice cracked and dry with the lilt of someone who mostly spoke Yiddish. But his tone was halting, accusatory. It said that the old man was certain the entire world was out to get the Jews, to hold them down and to persecute them. He was just waiting for Eli to prove him right. Insular and paranoid—calling cards of a cult.

"I'm here to make Shivah," Eli said simply. He could explain who he was, that he was family. But he didn't want to. He didn't want to claim anything more than the barest brush with this place and his past. Using Shivah, the tradition of visiting the grieving family and bringing food and comfort, should be enough to let him pass unmolested. But the old man resisted. He looked down at Eli's empty hands, his jeans and mixed fabric jacket, and then back at Eli's face, as if trying to discern how any goy would be so brazen as to claim to understand Jewish tradition.

"Ah, you know the family? Shivah has not begun, as the deceased has not had his funeral," the man pressed, unwilling to trust the outsider into his enclave.

Eli considered just turning around and leaving. Every step of this little sojourn was a mistake, and every chance it gave him to turn tail and flee was a missed opportunity.

"Yeah," Eli finally answered. "But I'm Eli, Elijah Rosenbaum. Dovev was my brother. I was asked to come."

18

It took the old man a moment to process Eli's answer, but when he did, his eyes widened in surprise and he scanned Eli's clothes and clean shaved face again. He had two options: call Eli a liar and continue to deny him entrance, or swallow his own pride and step aside. After several moments, he chose the latter and stepped back and away. Eli looked around one last time before stepping forward. Past the point of no return. He had pushed through the portal into his past.

2

The apartment hallway stretched into darkness, the only light coming through the windows. Each door, an entrance to a family home, was open, allowing full access to people's lives and privacy. It was a nest, a hive. Communal living that was both familiar and alien to Eli. He hadn't seen his brother or spoken to anyone in his family in so long, it all felt dreamlike. He had intended to walk straight back, eyes forward, ignoring all distractions and fulfilling what few familial obligations he felt he had to in order to avoid regret or guilt in the years to come. From the doorways, he could hear snatches of whispers, wordless in their quietness. Catching movement out of the corner of his eye, Eli turned, almost on instinct, following the flitting white shape as it passed through a room beyond one of the open doorways. He caught the impression of a white slip, clinging and flowing around an enticing leg and ass, but it was gone before he could really register it.

He turned back towards his destination and let out a startled yelp as a severe looking woman seemed to materialize out of the gloom in front of him. He took a step back, already turning red from embarrassment. He was just too busy trying to catch a look at someone's body and hadn't been looking where he was going. Eli forced himself to stand his ground and meet the woman's eyes. She stared back. Her eyes were cold, angry, and carried a pain that chipped away at his defenses.

Finally, he forced himself to speak.

"Hi, Ima," he greeted his mother, the Hebrew word sitting heavy on his tongue.

"Elijah," she said flatly. She took him in, his shoes, socks, jacket, and face. She sighed and stepped forward, straightening his collar and brushing his face. Her fingers trembled as though she were afraid he would brush them away, turn around and disappear as he had so long ago.

Eli stared at his mother as she fretted over him, taking him back to his Bar Mitzvah. Her hands were warm, her skin was soft, and despite how badly he wanted to not have any emotional response to her, he couldn't help but find some relief in a mother's care.

Finally, he stepped back, retreating from the love he had been rejecting for so long. "How are …?" He paused. That was a stupid question. Her son was dead; that's how she was doing. One of her sons, anyway—Eli supposed they had accepted him as dead to them long ago. Maybe he shouldn't have come at all; maybe coming was just reopening old wounds. "How is everyone? Is everyone holding up?" he finished lamely.

She shook her head and turned back towards the darkness. The whispers from the surrounding rooms seem to swell, growing louder but no more distinct. His mother didn't react to the sound crashing through the hallway like a physical force. She turned and looked over her shoulder at him. As their eyes met, the noise fell away. "Come. Elijah, come be with your family," she commanded before walking back into the gloom.

Eli glanced back and saw the woman he had glimpsed previously standing in the doorway staring at him. She was breathtaking. Her pale skin seemed to illuminate the surrounding shadows, and her dark eyes met his with so much promise that it made him gasp. She was slender, almost waifish, but her simple slip highlighted her slight curves and femininity. Her nipples pushed at the thin fabric, leaving little to his imagination. The shadows that did touch her created valleys that one could fall into. Perhaps it was just the sight of an attractive woman in what amounted to underwear in a place where modesty and sexlessness ruled that solicited such a reaction from him. But he was entranced.

"Elijah!"

He heard his name called from behind him and turned to look where his mother had gone, but she had been swallowed by the shadows. He turned back, eager to at least get the woman's name, but she, too, was gone, the door of the apartment, 109b, closed. He was alone in this dark hallway, accompanied only by the whispered prayers that seemed all the more ominous for their indistinct meaning.

He hurried in the direction his mother had gone.

After washing his hands using the bowl and pitcher of water just outside, Eli stepped through the doorway into his family's apartment. It was lit only by large candles here and there, with a box of more sitting next to a matchbox on top of a stool just inside. The smell of pickled cabbage pricked his nose, stinging his senses. He had avoided sauerkraut after leaving home. The smells brought with them something else. Memories of his time growing up here. He tried to focus on the memories of his siblings, which, to him, were the least offensive—playing with his brother, Dovev, or teasing his younger sister, Lilah, about whatever crush she had that week. Those were the good moments, the minutes between the crushing weight of expectation of stifling traditions.

Eli picked up one of the candles, turning it over in his hands for a moment before striking a match and lighting it. He carried it with him into the kitchen. Lilah was there, sitting at the kitchen counter, staring at him like he was a ghost that was intruding on her most private moments. He supposed that was accurate. He hadn't seen her in so long, hadn't been there for her wedding, or the birth of her children, or any other important time in her life. How did he deserve to be here?

His father, Erel, was standing near the sink. His fingers curled around the porcelain as though to hold him there. He was so old now. Was he holding himself up, or holding himself back from lashing out at his prodigal son? Eli was struck with the knowledge that his return, though his mother must have wanted it, was more painful; it reminded them that their loss was two-fold. That they had lost both sons. The air was thick with tension. He didn't even know how to greet his sister or father.

But something was odd, wrong. It took him several moments to realize what it was. Minutes where the tension just grew and increased, stretching to a near breaking point. Finally, he shattered the silence as he realized what was missing.

"Where is Dovev?" Eli asked, his voice seeming small and meaningless in the little kitchen. As he asked, he set the candle down on the counter, letting its light join the luminescence of the others in the room.

"At the coroner with Reb Kaltov," Erel said, the words cold and distant, devoid of emotion. But his father's voice was always like that, flat and emotionless, except during prayer. He reserved all of his joy and his boundless love for the words on a page to an unhearing, uncaring god, while his children were left to starve for fatherly affection that came neither from their earthly nor heavenly fathers.

"The coroner?" Eli repeated, confused. "Why is he there?" It went against Jewish law and custom for the body to undergo an autopsy. There were laws against a body being desecrated and other laws against being buried with any of your organs missing. Generally when someone passed, their body would be kept with the family until it could be buried, with someone standing vigil over the corpse the entire time to ensure no one violated it. That his father would allow for an autopsy was bizarre and unnerving. For him to send another rabbi to oversee it felt even more alien.

"He was murdered, Eli." Lilah said the words softly, in a hushed tone that almost made the declaration gentle. It took Eli a few moments to register what she said.

"What?" He shouted the question, his voice filling not just the room but the entire apartment complex. No one spoke for a moment, letting the echo of his outburst fade in the darkness. Eli felt himself burning as blood flushed his face in embarrassment. "What happened?" he finally asked.

"If we knew the details or what happened," Erel muttered, "then your brother wouldn't be getting an autopsy." After a few more moments of awkward silence, Erel looked up from his vigil over the porcelain sink at his son and nodded. "Welcome home, Elijah." His eyes behind his glasses were huge, highlighting the wateriness and cataracts, as well as the dark circles from sleeplessness. They traveled over Eli, taking in his secular dress. He was a disappointment to his father, but that was nothing new.

"Hey, Aba," Elijah returned the greeting. "Hi, Lilah," he finished lamely to his sister.

25

They fell back into a crushing silence. Was the awkwardness and lack of warmth and sound because of his presence? Was he reading too much into a family that had just lost one of their own to murder? Or was it always like this, and the stillness just seemed oppressive because he had grown so used to the noise and chaos outside of these walls? Doom pressed all around; it hung in the air as though the Sameal that he had grown up fearing as the angel of death was in the room, towering over them, spreading his wings like a canopy to entomb them.

Eli shook the thought off and stepped past his father and sister to walk down the hall and stand before the door of the room he had once shared with Dovev. The door was slightly ajar. Eli put his hand to his lips and reached up to brush his fingertips against the mezuzah there. It was instinct, an empty gesture, but one he hoped would maybe pay some respect to his watching family. He pushed the door open and stared into the dark room.

The shifting shadows and growing light told him that someone had brought a candle from the kitchen as they walked towards him. The light brought with it new information. The room was nothing like he had left it, and why would it be? It was obvious Dovev had continued living here. It was the room of a single bachelor, a man who had yet to find a wife in a community that stressed the importance of marriage. Eli had been so furious after his Bar Mitzvah that Dovev would be staying in his room. He wasn't a little kid anymore; he shouldn't share his room with a child!

Eli stepped into the room, looking around at all the little things his brother had kept. "Why didn't Dovev get married?" he asked, reaching over to run his fingers over the worn and dog-eared copy of a siddur, feeling the embossed Hebrew letters of the cover.

"Dovev didn't have a lot of interest in that sort of thing," Lilah said. "About as much interest in finding a wife as you had in …" She trailed off and gestured at the room around her.

"What? Living here?" he asked.

"Being family is what I was trying to say," she clarified. "He wanted to start a family like you wanted to be part of ours."

"Ah." Eli glanced over his shoulder at her. She wasn't wrong, but he had expected the venom and accusations to come from his father, the guilt trip to come from his mother, not from Lilah. She had been so young when he left, he was surprised she recognized him at all, or even cared about whether he had stayed or left. He stepped across the room, looking over the posters and various decor items.

"Was it really so bad?" Lilah asked from the doorway, setting the candle down. "Couldn't you have stayed? For Dovev? For me?"

Eli didn't know what to say. "I couldn't stay here. It was suffocating; it's not who I am."

There was silence for a long moment as Eli looked through his brother's life. He paused as something caught his eye. Lifting the mattress of his brother's bed, he saw several men's fitness magazines hidden between the mattress and the boxsprings. Muscular, oiled, airbrushed men smiled up from the covers at him. Articles promising prowess at sex and becoming irresistible shouted at him in bold fonts.

"A lot of us have to be things we aren't. A lot of us don't have the strength to leave on our own," she said.

Dovev wanted to be, what? A body builder? Eli fumbled at the thought; he had never been what anyone would call overly masculine. He glanced at Lilah to ask what she meant, but she just shook her head.

"I'm sure you were planning on stopping by and then leaving again, but you should stay till the funeral at least."

Eli turned away. It was hard to meet her eyes, looking for the words to say no, looking for a good excuse that he could believe himself. But he was coming up empty. He was still trying to discern why Dovev was keeping muscle mags under his mattress and what Lilah had meant. Before he could think of a response, though, he heard his mother's voice from the kitchen, calling them for dinner.

3

Eli lay in his brother's bed, the lone candle he had brought into the house illuminating the ceiling. After a dinner of bland casserole brought by a neighbor—coming home didn't even confer the reward of a mom-cooked meal—he had retreated to the bedroom.

He had tooled around on his phone for a bit, explaining to his girlfriend, Cynthia, why he wasn't coming home immediately. She had wanted to call, to console him, but he promised he was okay and that they would talk tomorrow when he had his "head on straight." He promised he would be home in time for Christmas and then flipped through social media for an hour, hoping the drudgery of the world would help lull him into a sense of comfort that would allow him to fall asleep. When he was done scrolling as much as he could stand, he tossed his phone aside and stared at the ceiling, waiting for sleep to take him.

Eli's eyes were just starting to get heavy when he heard the door opening. He shot upright, wondering which parent had decided that the middle of the night was the right time to start a fight. To his surprise, it wasn't his mom, father, or even Lilah; it was the girl from the hallway.

She hadn't changed, the shimmering pearl of her slip seeming to refract light into rainbows in the dim candlelight. Her white skin seemed to glow in the gloom of the room as she turned, closed the door, and turned to face him. Long, black, wavy hair framed her slender face, casting shadows across her features. But he could see her smile; it was full of promise and mischief.

"What are you doing in here?" Eli whispered.

He started to get up, but stopped, as she was suddenly standing over him, her hand on his shoulder, pushing him back down. Her other hand was raised to her face, a single digit extended to her lips, shushing him. He noticed her hand on his shoulder was wet, but he couldn't take his eyes off her face. He raised an eyebrow in question as she used her leg to push the covers off of Eli and climbed onto the bed, hiked up her slip, and straddled him.

His mind reeled. What was happening? This girl had broken into his family's home, found him, and was … His mind blanked as he felt her thighs squeezing him. She locked eyes with Eli as she rocked on top of him. He could feel the shape of her against him through the thin fabric of his pajama pants. He should stop this. It wasn't right. He didn't know her, he had a girlfriend, and even if both of those things were untrue, he was laying in his dead brother's bed. He couldn't fuck here.

But his body wasn't listening to him. It only felt the warmth from the woman spreading over him. He could hear her panting, breathing hard as she ground down on top of him. She reached down, lifting off him for a moment to reach under the elastic of his pants and pull him free. Eli gasped at the cool sensation of her hand gripping him. This was it, his last chance to protest before it was too late. In his heart, he knew it was already too late, this had already gone too far; he knew he wouldn't stop it.

She smiled down at him, her hand stroking up and down before tightening her grip to guide Eli into her. She lowered herself back down over him. Her skin was cool, but inside her, it was warm and inviting. Eli clenched his ass, lifting himself off the bed and pushing deeper into her. She writhed on him, her entire body undulating in sinuous motion. It was the most beautiful sex he could imagine. Every time he'd had sex, it had been a panicked rush, a race to try to get his partner off before he came. He was always so concerned with trying to be good that the act itself was nothing more than a frenzy. But not this. This was completely different.

As she moved on top of him like some weightless dancer, he reached up, his hands running over her hips and sides. The slip was warm and wet under his hands; he dismissed it as sweat. He closed his eyes for a moment, continuing to explore her body through the wet fabric of her nightie. He could feel himself getting close. He wanted to see her; he wanted to reach his own climax staring at her face.

31

He opened his eyes and saw that she was drenched, not in sweat but in some dark, sticky wetness. He turned, lifted his hand from her breast, and turned it towards the candle to see what was on him, but the girl grabbed his wrist and forced it down to the bed, pinning both of his arms over his head as she quickened her pace. She slammed down on him, pushing him into the bed. Her face inches from his as she fucked him into submission, he could see the wetness, whatever it was, coated the bottom half of her face. He couldn't focus on it, couldn't concentrate on anything as she released him and arched her back, pulling an orgasm out of him that rocked through his body in a way he had never experienced before. He collapsed back onto the bed, delirious and panting, and passed out.

Eli awoke with a start, jolting upright in bed. It took him several minutes to remember where he was. The room was pitch black. Eli groped in the darkness to find his phone and hit the flashlight app. The sudden brightness hurt his eyes, and he squinted against it. He fell back into the bed and rubbed his face, trying to massage the haze from his mind. His hand was wet and sticky.

Immediately, he remembered the dream; the girl, the sex, the wetness. It had been so intense, and he became aware that he could feel the after-buzz of a great orgasm. Realizing he must have cum in his sleep and just rubbed his face, Eli groaned in disgust and rose to emerge from the room to sneak to the bathroom and clean himself off. Once inside the bathroom with the door locked, Eli turned on the light and turned to face the mirror. It was all he could do to stifle his yelp of surprise. There was a large dark-red streak across his face and several red handprints on his chest. He dragged a finger through the mark and pulled his hand away. Both of his hands were coated in the red stuff. Looking down, he saw a large smear of it on his belly disappearing under his pajama pants.

Almost panicked, he turned on the water and began trying to rinse it off his hands. It was blood, he knew it was blood, what else could it be? Where did it come from? Did he leave a lot of blood on his brother's bed? Was he hurt? A million questions slammed through Eli's mind as he grabbed the soap and vigorously washed himself in the sink, trying to get all of the blood off. He didn't hurt; almost the opposite, the incredible sexy dream had left him feeling good. He was still tingling, but his anxiety over finding so much blood on him was ruining that quickly. After several minutes of hurried scrubbing at his skin, he managed to clean it off.

He spent several more minutes wiping down the bathroom, cleaning up the spots that had landed on the sink and mirror. His skin was raw from scrubbing, and the little hand towel he had used was an awful shade of pink. He was about to sneak back to Dov's room when a terrified scream tore through the thin walls.

Eli nearly jumped out of his skin, his heart pounding in his chest hard enough to make his ribs ache. As the scream died, he could hear his parents and family stirring. Panicked at being caught, Eli darted back into the bedroom and quickly stripped, pushing the rag and his pants under the mattress next to the magazines. He rushed to pull open his suitcase and got dressed as quickly as possible. He was still pulling on his shirt when he pushed open the door and stepped out to join his dad and mom in the hallway.

"What's going on?" he asked, sure they didn't know more than he did but trying to sound innocent himself, not even sure where his guilt was coming from.

"How should I know what is going on?" his father asked, pushing forward and past Eli towards the door.

Eli followed, glancing back at his mother. She didn't look scared, as he would expect, but tired and frustrated. Her lips were pressed together in a grim line. She met his eyes. There was no fear there, just the haggard and defeated gaze of a woman who had lost her son.

"Go," she said. "I will check on Lilah." She turned and disappeared down the hall towards his sister's room.

Eli watched her for a moment and then rushed after his father, his curiosity about what had happened overwhelming his sense of distaste for the man and making him all but forget about the strange dream and blood for the moment. Out in the hallways, the residents of the apartments were coming out in droves, summoned by the scream that had shaken the entire building. People were gathering outside of apartment 109b. The apartment he had seen the woman in yesterday.

Eli's dream came crashing back to the front of his mind. The bloody residue on his body occupied his full attention as he forced his way to the front of the group, jostling those around him. The door was closed. Without thinking about it, he raised his fist and pummeled the door. "Hello! Is everyone all right in there?"

After a few seconds, the door was flung open, and a sobbing middle-aged woman stood there, sweating and terrified. Even in the gloom, Eli could see the blood splatter on her face. Wordlessly, gasping for breath around her tears, she stepped aside and let him in. The Chassidim followed behind him. He could hear their murmuring, the fear in their voices, the supposition of what could be happening. Already, he could hear someone muttering a useless prayer.

Eli pushed forward, ignoring the sounds behind him. His eyes and his full attention were locked on the trail of blood drops the woman had shed on her way to the door. What would he find? He was terrified as he approached the doorway the blood led him to. His entire psyche was poised, ready to find his nocturnal lover there, dead and cut into pieces like the Black

35

Dhalia.

He pushed into light of the room and almost fell back as he found the source of the bloody mess. Lying in the bed was an old man, his eyes frozen wide in terror. His jaw had been ripped off, and bloody claw marks had been torn through his chest and stomach. There was blood everywhere, and Eli could see remnants of intestine lying in tattered loops on the bed. He turned and vomited.

He could smell the blood and shit. There was gore was everywhere—like a Jackson Pollack painting in bloodstained feces. He closed his eyes as he stumbled to the side of the door and tried to catch his breath. Others were following him into the room, shouting as they discovered what was there. The prayers and cries filled Eli's head, making the room even more claustrophobic. Whatever had happened in this room, it was monstrous. The man had been savaged worse than anything Eli had seen before. It looked like he had been the victim of some industrial accident, or as if a bear had gotten into the room and attacked.

Eli stepped back, trying to retreat despite the throng of people trying to get in. His foot hit something, and looking down, Eli saw a small box on the floor. He had kicked it and knocked it open. It pulled at his attention, a focal point for his attention within the maelstrom of the room. With all the noise, chaos, and blood around him, he hyper focused on the box. It looked like one of the old wooden cigar boxes with the hinged top that you would find at a liquor store. A layer of multicolored wax covered it, as though someone had melted a dozen candles on it over the years. Next to the box, scattered from when he kicked it, were ashes and little pieces of bric-a-brac. Eli could make out foil wrapped gelt, ashes, a birthday cake candle, and what looked like human teeth.

He was about to bend over and pick up the box when someone bumped into him, knocking him over. Eli looked up at the older man, who glared at him. Realizing how weird it would be to pick up someone else's property at the scene of a murder, Eli rose and brushed himself off, pushing through the crowd to get out of the room. As he sought to untangle himself from the throng, he saw his mother consoling the sobbing woman; she looked grim. Eli avoided making eye contact with her or anyone else as he made his way back to his family's apartment, the sound of sirens already growing louder in the distance.

He didn't notice the dark eyes of the slender woman watching him from the doorway of the next apartment over.

MONDAY

4

The four of them sat around the kitchen table. Eli's mother, Ruth, was making eggs and toast for everyone. Eli watched in silence for several minutes. Ruth fried an egg, then served Lilah, and then Erel. She started to clean then skillet and then paused, turning to Eli. She looked upset, more upset now than she had looked in the apartment of the murdered man.

"How do you like your eggs, Elijah?" she asked.

Eli frowned. Had she been about to make eggs for Dovev? Eli wanted to tell her that he liked his eggs with bacon, bacon and extra cheese. Eli wanted to lash out at them still, to hurt them. He didn't even have a good reason other than being angry that his life was disrupted. That made his chest hurt. He was more upset that he had to be here with his family than he was sad that his brother was dead.

"Scrambled" he muttered, but then something else occurred to him "Wait, you said that Dovev was killed. Was that how he was killed? Torn apart!?" Eli hadn't meant to shout, but it came out so much louder than he intended.

Erel and Ruth glanced at each other, and Eli imagined there was venom in that look, that there was something other than a parent's pain.

"Don't be foolish," Erel finally answered, turning his eyes away from his wife. "You slept in the bed. Did it look like someone had been ..." He gestured vaguely in the direction of apartment 109b.

A look of pure rage passed Ruth's face. She tried to hide it, turning back to the stove to crack two more eggs into the skillet. Eli assumed it was because he was asking for details from a family that was intensely private, even to one of their own. But a second later, what his dad had said registered.

"Wait? What? Dovev died in his bed?"

"Don't shout," his mother chided.

"Don't shout!" Eli shouted. "Are you kidding me? My brother died in that bed, was murdered, and you're just having me sleep in there like nothing is wrong?" The sound of people moving outside the apartment reminded Eli that the cops were everywhere, swarming over the little complex like ants whose nest had been disturbed. But they weren't. The Jews who sat calmly while their friends were killed and their lives disrupted were the ants of this hill. The cops were just intruders. Eli had to wonder what they were more interested in, solving the crime or the spectacle of the brutal murder and oddly behaving Chassidim.

Either way, it reminded him to lower his voice. "You didn't even tell me," Eli finished lamely.

There were a few moments of silence. "Well, you know now. You can sleep on the couch," Erel said gruffly.

They fell into silence again. The smell of coffee and the sound of eggs sizzling in the pan were the only things that remained after the echoes of speech faded. Eli stared down into the coffee in front of him, black, no cream. He hated it, but he needed the caffeine.

Sleeping in the bed his brother was murdered in … and his parents had let him—it said something about how much they gave a shit about it. And he had that sex dream in his dead brother's bed. That dream. Eli swallowed, getting hot as he thought about the dream. It had been so intense, so powerful. His skin tingled, his brain felt hot, and he could feel himself getting aroused. He tried to force his mind back to the matter at hand, but it just kept going back to the way the woman's body had writhed on top of him. Eli coughed. What if he had that dream again? Waking up and seeing blood had been terrifying. But with as wound up as he felt now, the idea of not being able to squeeze one off before he laid down made him feel like he would never fall asleep.

"Uh—no," he finally stuttered. "It's fine. I'll sleep in his room," he said lamely as his mother set the eggs down in front of him. They smelled good. But bland. He preferred his eggs cooked with bacon grease and smothered in cheese. He pushed the eggs around his plate for a moment. He should never have come back here.

No one argued with him about the room, or even questioned it. He didn't know if it was because they didn't care or if they just disliked him enough to not want to talk to him about it.

A moment later, the silent gloom that had descended on the room was interrupted by a knock on the door. It was their turn to deal with the cops. Eli looked up, watching his father rise and make his way to the door, leaving his teffilin and siddur on the table, more concerned with when he would be able to get to his prayers than the tragedy all around him.

Eli listened to his father speaking to the police. His low voice was audible but not loud enough to make out the words he spoke in hushed tones. The cop, his voice less tempered with respect for the dead, was perfectly audible.

"Yes, I understand that," the cop was saying in between murmurs from his father. "Well, I don't know." A pause. "Yes, I understand that. I can check with the coroner, but you have to understand this is extenuating circumstances as is." Another pause. "Yes, your rabbi friend is still with your son." This time, the pause from the officer was longer while Erel grumbled through several thoughts. Eli wished he could understand what was being said.

41

Then, "You said you're other son is here? When did he get here?"

Eli frowned at the question—why was he being brought into this? A second later, though, his father and the policeman rounded the corner from the entryway. Erel gestured at Eli, as though offering Isaac up on the mountain. Though there would be no gift from god to take his place.

"Elijah Rosenbaum, I'm Lt. Spence with Brooklyn PD," the cop was saying. He was a younger guy, probably no older than Eli himself. He had an air of trying to project authority and failing miserably—Eli could relate.

"Um, okay, hi," Eli responded, unsure of why he was now being forced to converse with the cops.

"Your dad tells me you just got into town? That this was your first night here?" The questions would be friendly if they weren't being asked by a cop in the middle of a murder investigation.

"Uh ..." Eli sputtered, looking between Erel and Spence. "Uh, yeah."

"So you weren't in town when your brother died?" Spence asked, his eyebrows shooting up.

"Wait, are you asking where I was when my brother was killed? Are you accusing me of having something to do with that?" Eli asked.

"That's preposterous," his mother cut in. "He wasn't even

42

here. He was in California." Erel shot her a look, but she ignored it. "Tell him," she urged Eli.

Eli paused. He was surprised his mother knew where he had been living; he was also embarrassed he had to contradict her when she was defending him. "Uh, no, I was in New York, but I was in Manhattan, at a conference," he said, but then frowned. "I'm sorry, am I a suspect?" Eli didn't look at his mom; he didn't want to address the fact that he came to New York several times over the last few years and had never, in all of those visits, even checked in on his family.

Spence's lips pressed together in a tight line, but Eli could see the malice lurking in his eyes. He was the sort of person who delighted when other people failed. He didn't want to stop a crime or help people; he wanted to be justified in punishing them. He wanted Eli to be guilty; he wanted to catch Eli. Spence visibly swallowed his excitement, seeming to remember himself.

"No, of course not, just standard procedure. Can anyone verify where you were at the time of the attack last night?"

Eli glanced at his father; he didn't seem overly concerned, maybe even a little relieved to not be talking to the goy policeman. Lilah and his mother both looked angry, glaring daggers silently at the officer. At least they, in some small way, had his back. At least they cared more about the truth and their family than their own comfort, even if they wouldn't say

43

anything out loud.

"I was in bed, here."

"Can anyone confirm that?"

"What? No, everyone was asleep, including me," Eli protested, but his mind wound back to the dream, to the woman who had rode him so passionately in his sleep that it felt like reality.

"Right, so no one can confirm where you were last night? What about three nights ago?" Spence asked. He had looped back to asking about Dovev.

Eli's head was spinning. He wasn't sure if he should even answer the questions that this cop was asking. But if he asked for a lawyer ... well, wouldn't that just make him look more guilty? Was there any way out of this?

"Uh, yeah, I'm sure any of the sales team could vouch for me," Eli finally said uncertainly. Would they? He had no idea, but it was the best he had.

"Great." Officer Spence did not look like he was happy to hear someone could provide an alibi. He looked like he had eaten something disappointing. "You have their contact information?"

"Yup," Eli said, digging his phone out of his back pocket. *Fuck this*, he thought then. As soon as this asshole left, he would too, call an uber and head back home to California. He didn't owe his family anything, he definitely didn't owe them being

44

thrown under the bus of a fucking murder investigation. He grabbed the offered pencil and paper from the officer and starting writing down the names of his team members he had come to New York with, his full attention on getting out of this as quickly as possible and going back home.

"Okay, so these people can vouch for your whereabouts over the last few days?" Lt. Spence asked.

"They should be able to, yeah," Eli agreed before setting down the pencil. "They were all at the same conference I was at, so ..." He trailed off, hoping the cop would get the message and leave so he could pack and get the fuck out of here too.

"So, you'll be here," Spence said—it was framed like a question, but Eli could tell it was a statement, an order.

"Well actually I need to get back to work, back ho—"

"We would prefer if you not leave town, actually." Spence cut him off.

Eli frowned. Though he didn't look back, he could tell his sister and mother were staring at him. They had wanted him to stay for the funeral anyway, probably felt betrayed when he said he wanted to leave. He could still see that malicious glee in the cop's eyes. He enjoyed this part. Even if Eli was innocent, he was happy to bully someone, to inconvenience them. He would probably go home and jack off to the thought of Eli losing his job because he couldn't go back to California.

As annoyed as he was, though, there was something in the

back of his head, some relief. He could maybe see the woman he had seen again, maybe speak to her, maybe dream again. As soon as that thought crossed his mind, he blushed, feeling guilty and embarrassed about being excited for some wet dream. "I uh … I was going to be staying for Dovev's funeral anyway, so … I'll be here that long, anyway," Eli mumbled, trying to assert some authority into his own life again.

"Sounds good. We'll be in touch, Mr. Rosenbaum." Spence tipped his hat to the women and walked out of the kitchen.

Eli deflated a little and looked around the room at his mother and sister, pointedly ignoring his father. It was his fault. His dad had decided to bring Eli into this, and now, because he had decided to come and see his family, he was suspected of murder. It was just more evidence that he should never have come in the first place. He rose and moved to Dovev's room.

"I'm going to get some work done," he said before shutting the door behind him and grabbing his laptop.

5

Work was easy. They were close enough to the holidays that most people were taking breaks and vacations, and so his queue was nearly empty, even with having been out of pocket for nearly a week But his family didn't need to know that. They didn't need to know that after a few moments of noodling around on his laptop, he had shut it and lifted the mattress to find the bloody clothes he had hidden there, next to the magazines that had made the hiding spot their home for ... well, who knew how long.

The magazines. Eli picked up the magazines and dropped the mattress. This was a different mystery. Why did Dovev have these under his mattress? He flipped one open and turned over a couple of pages. Men's magazines had always made him laugh; they were all essentially porn. Men's interest rags were filled with pictures of actresses in underwear with tips for getting laid, and these fitness magazines were hardly any better. The sheer homoeroticism of them was almost over the top. Eli pulled two pages apart that stuck together, almost as if they had been glued. It actually made him laugh out loud—magazines hidden in the mattress, pages stuck together like ...

Eli tossed the magazine away from him like it had bitten

him. What had been humorous moments ago now seemed like a ghastly certainty. These magazines were Dovev's porn stash. He had sat in this room, hidden away from his parents, and jacked off while staring at oiled-down muscle men. He thought back to what his sister had said just yesterday, about people having to be things that they weren't. The thought of being gay in a fundamentalist household, especially *this* fundamentalism household, was heartbreaking.

Dovev had hidden himself back here and fantasized about being free, about being able to be himself. Eli stood and grabbed the magazine he had thrown when he realized he was probably touching his brother's dried cum-rag. He looked at the cover for a moment, his heart hurting at how lonely his little brother must have felt. After a moment, he rummaged through the room, grabbing all the magazines he could find. He opened draws, checked the back of the closet, anywhere he could think of that someone might try to hide pornography or themselves.

It was the only way he could help Dovev now. It was the equivalent of deleting his browser history. He shoved all the magazines in his backpack—he would throw them out when he could, but now, at least, Dovev wouldn't have to go through a postmortem scandal. Eli sat back down on the bed, looking around the room with a new apprehension. He had spent so much of his life hating this place for being a stifling hell, but what did that mean? It meant he couldn't play violent video games; it meant he had been forced to pray and go to the synagogue all the time. But in the end, that was really the worst of it for him.

What sort of torture had Dovev been going through? And what had happened to him? Lilah had said he was murdered, but there were no signs of struggle or violence in the room. Eli sighed and tossed his backpack in the corner of the room. As much as he wanted to just stay here, locked away until later, he wanted to get more information. He slowly opened the door and peered around the corner, feeling like a teenager sneaking out of the house. It wasn't that different, only instead of trying to avoid his father so he could go down the street and catch a train to play Smash Brothers with the goyim, he was trying to avoid his dad so he could ask his sister what the fuck had happened to Dovev.

The coast was clear. Aba was probably out in the hallway talking to neighbors or at shul. He could see his mother in the kitchen. It felt like he had stepped back in time for a moment, until he saw his sister sitting quietly in the living room. She was still a kid to him in a lot of ways, but she wasn't the little girl he had abandoned. The thought slapped him. He had abandoned her, like Dovev. Life couldn't be better for her here than it had been for him. He walked towards her and collapsed into the couch, feeling sheepish, weak, and cruel.

"Hey," he muttered.

"Hey," she said back.

He didn't know her. She had been seven when he ran off to join the real world, but he remembered how she had been then: kind, sweet, annoying in how she clung to him and Dovev. It made his heart hurt more—she had loved him, truly loved him and looked up to him, and then he had one day, without warning or even a goodbye, disappeared.

"I'm sorry," he finally said ineffectually.

"For?" The word was pointed. They both knew all the things he needed to be sorry for; she just doubted he had the capacity to understand how badly he had fucked up, how badly he had screwed her over.

"Everything, leaving. Leaving you and Dov." Eli stared down at his hands. He hated the feeling in the pit of his stomach. He had sustained himself on hate and rage for the past decade. Every time he thought about home, he thought about how much he hated his father, hated the stifling religious community. He hated how it seemed to come so easy to other boys and how alien it felt to him. He never thought about his mother's tenderness; he never thought about his brother or sister. That realization hurt. It hurt worse knowing he could never speak to or apologize to Dovev.

"Did you think about coming back? Did you think about us?" Lilah asked.

"Yes," he lied. "But I knew I couldn't come back. Aba

wouldn't have accepted me coming back, especially after I abandoned religion." He wanted to say more, but everything he said was a lie, no sense in digging further holes. "I'm sorry."

"Religion—is that all you think you abandoned?" she asked. "You also abandoned your culture, your history, your people, your identity—"

"It was never the identity I wanted; it was the one I was given."

"And you threw it away with everything else. Including your family." She rose to leave, but Eli caught her hand.

"Yes, I did. But I was suffocating here. I just didn't know Dovev was. I didn't know you would." Lilah looked down at their hands and pulled back, freeing herself. "What really happened to Dov, Lilah?" Eli asked, slowly dropping his hand.

"What is there to say? He's dead."

"How? How was he killed?" Eli pressed.

Lilah stared at him, the hard anger in her eyes slowly falling away into sadness, dismay, regret. "He was … poisoned. Sleeping pills." She shrugged. "I heard him choking and found him …" She shook her head, tears welling up in her eyes. "Killed. The only thing that *killed* him was being alone, Eli. If you want to know who the murderer is, Aba is somewhere around here and there's a mirror in the bathroom." She turned and left.

Eli was too stunned, too hurt, to move from the spot.

51

A few minutes later, his mother came in. She didn't say anything, simply walked across the room, picking up, dusting. She didn't meet Eli's eyes; she didn't even acknowledge him. For a moment, he felt like he was the one who died instead of Dovev, like he was a ghost, a dybbuk in this place, haunting it and hurting the occupants by his mere presence.

After a few minutes, he got up from the couch and made himself a sandwich in the kitchen. Everything was where it had been ten years ago. He tried to work up some of his old outrage, tried to tap into the disgust he felt for his parents and for this community. But it lay dead in his heart like the rotting corpse of a deer on the side of the road. Lilah was as trapped as he was a decade ago, maybe their mother was too. Dovev was the only one who had escaped. Eli sat at the table alone and ate his sandwich in silence.

He wanted to feel relief that his brother wasn't torn apart like the old man in 109b, but all he could think of was how terribly isolated Dovev must have been. Eli considered himself politically agnostic. But he was a straight white guy working in tech; he didn't *need* to pay attention to politics. He didn't *need* to care. Suddenly, he cared, now that it affected him, or had affected him, anyway. His brother was gay. His brother was gay, and stupid religious and political bullshit had made him kill himself.

Eli caught himself. This was the cycle of grief; he was at

anger. Was he angry that Dovev was dead, or at why Dovev was dead? Or maybe he was angry that his sister was laying that guilt at his feet. But she wasn't wrong, was she? He considered going and knocking on her door, asking her to talk, trying to make things better, but with Dovev gone and it being at least partially his fault, things could never be better again, could they? Dovev had freed himself and effectively destroyed any chance of reconciliation all at once. Not that he had ever thought that would be something he wanted. He still didn't want it. He still hated this place, this community. He still wanted to be free. He just wanted to lie in bed and dream about that woman …

That brought him up short. The fuck? No, he wanted to go home and see his girlfriend. He wanted to open whatever silly present she got him and then watch whatever dumb Christmas movies were on TV. He wanted to distance himself from his family, his people, his Jewish identity as much as possible. He rose from the table and made his way to Dovev's bedroom. There was nothing for him here. All he could do was wait to be freed of his obligations and leave it behind forever.

Eli sat on the bed and pushed open his laptop. He spent a few moments clicking between various work applications. Slack, Asana, Monday, Teams, Airtable, Jira … a thousand project management tools spread between a hundred project managers, used to manage four engineers. He had gotten through the small list of work items for the current sprint, and normally, he would be happy with that. He could say he did his work and go about his life, watch TV, play video games, whatever the hell he wanted for the rest of the day.

But there was none of that here. Sure, he could leave the house, hop on a train, and go to a different part of the city—it wasn't like he didn't know people living in New York—it just felt pointless. Working to kill time. A new low for him, but he didn't want to doom scroll on his phone, and there was no point in trying to make amends with his family. His heart ached at the pain he had caused, but there was no balm for that now. Nothing that could help.

So instead, Eli buried himself in mindless coding. Some of the other engineers bitched about the way the executives flip-flopped back and forth on design and requests, complaining that it was a waste of time, that most of it was bizarre cosmetic choices that would be undone next sprint or ludicrous requests that would be a nightmare to implement. Eli didn't care. These sort of nonvital requests were perfect for when he wanted low-stakes projects. He could take all the time he wanted on these projects because no one actually cared other than the executive pushing it, but by the time Eli finished with them, those same executives would be on to their next shiny idea.

He pulled up his code editor and began to work, pulling together the necessary threads to implement the ludicrous suggestion that the "subscribe" button move around the screen, forcing people to chase it to click it. The current CEO had suggested that after reading an article on "gamifying user experience." Was it a terrible idea? Yes. Was it a waste of time? Yes. But if he was working on it, no one could claim he wasn't doing his job. It was almost zen, coding line after line, testing in the closed environment, and then going back to write more code.

He could have probably kept working on the code all night but was interrupted by a knock on the door.

"Yeah?" he asked, not taking his eyes off his screen.

"Dinner," Lilah's voice called.

"Coming," Eli called back, saving his work and closing his laptop. He wasn't looking forward to the awkward kosher meal around the table. He stretched, working out the stiffness caused by hours of hunching over his laptop, before walking to the door and opening it. He was surprised to find Lilah still standing there.

"Uh … hey," he said awkwardly.

"Hey. I … I'm sorry. About earlier," she muttered, a slight blush coloring her cheeks.

"You don't have to apologize."

"I do. You didn't deserve that. I'm just so angry. Dov—"

"Didn't deserve this either. I get that you're angry. That you blame me."

"I'm angry that you didn't take us with you. That you left us to this. I love our parents, Eli; I love G-d. But ... I feel like I'm only experiencing a singular slice of life, like I don't even know what I'm missing. And that's better than Dov. He knew what he wanted, he knew what he needed, he just wasn't allowed to have it. I don't actually blame you for what happened. I blame men like Aba. I blame the rules and the stigma. I blame the idea that HaShem is angrier than he is loving."

"I don't know, I don't—" Eli floundered, trying to grasp for the words, how to tell his religious sister that the world was so much better once he abandoned superstition and the fantasy of faith.

"You don't believe," she finished. He shook his head. "Yeah, I figured. You know Aba and his friends, they call anyone who isn't Chassid 'not religious.' So I didn't know if you abandoned everything or just ... you know ... their version of it."

"Everything," Eli said softly. "I just couldn't see the good through the anger. I still can't. But ... I see you. I see Ima."

"But not Aba," she said. It wasn't a question.

"No. He still represents everything, every reason I left. He hasn't changed either. I hadn't expected him to, but ... No, I left behind all of that."

Lilah nodded. "When I was little, with you and Dov, I was happy. You know? Me and my big brothers. You protected me from the sadness and the anger that was here. Dovev did his best, but his own sadness was overwhelming to him. You ran away from it, but did you escape it?"

The question hung in the air. There was no malice in the question, no anger. He stood there, looking into his sister's eyes, wishing he could tell her that he was happy now, that everything was okay, that she could, if she wanted to, follow the same path and be a happy and free person. But he couldn't. The truth was the anger and anguish had followed him throughout his life and that, even now, he knew none of them would ever be truly free from it.

He said nothing, but she heard every word of his silence. She looked down, hiding her own sad tears, and nodded before wiping her eyes and turning to head into the dining room, not waiting for him to follow.

6

Dinner was just as awkward as he had expected it to be. A silent pall that was nearly suffocating. What made it worse was that Eli knew it was his fault. He had seen his father with his friends; they would laugh, sing, and pray at dinner. Eli shuffled the food around his plate. It wasn't bad—steak, potatoes, and spinach— but the necessities of a kosher kitchen meant the food was dry and overcooked, in Eli's opinion. He wondered if his family had ever tasted delicious cheesy mashed potatoes or a medium rare steak. Life's simple pleasures that he now took for granted.

"The funeral will be tomorrow," Erel said, shattering the silence so suddenly that Lilah started.

"The autopsy is done?" Eli asked.

"Why should it not be done? Would we have the funeral if it was not?" Erel asked.

Eli bit his tongue and stopped himself from rolling his eyes. He didn't know why his father spoke like a petulant teenager, but he didn't like it any more now than he had as a kid. He waited a moment, watching his father return to his food as though nothing was amiss.

"Okay, and what did they say?" Eli pressed.

"This is not a topic for dinner," Erel muttered.

"Oh, fuck off!" Eli said. The outburst caused Lilah to jump, while his mom looked absolutely shocked at the sudden profanity. Eli didn't care. "I don't care about dinner. I don't care about being proper or your rules. What I do care about is that my brother is dead. That's the only reason I'm here, the only reason we're around this table right now. So, I would like to know *how* my brother died, I would like to know when the funeral is, and then, hey, guess what?"

"You'll go back home," Lilah said softly, the only one who wasn't stunned into silence.

"No, Lilah, I won't. Because Aba here decided it would be a great idea to say something to the cops to make them think I murdered my own brother. So now, instead of getting me out of your hair, I have to stay here until the cops decide to clear me or, fuck, arrest me as an easy target."

"You think I was trying to get the police to attack you?" Erel spat. "How stupid can you be? You go out into the secular world, and you forget what decency is."

"The fact that you think that *you're* a decent person is—"

"No!" Erel roared. "You don't get to come into my home, you don't get to come back after so many years and pretend you are the victim. We mourn Dovev, my son, my *only* son, and you try to come in, and as with everything, you try to make it about yourself!"

Erel's words slammed into Eli like a solid force, knocking

the wind out of his chest. "Your only son," he repeated.

"What? You disowned us, boy. That was your decision. Did you think that you could hurt us like you hurt us and we would just sit in stasis? We prayed for you, every day. During the kaddish, I remembered my boy, my little boy. No, to me, you've been dead for ten years. You are a dybbuk haunting my home and memories. And you come in and make demands. You look at us with disdain because you think you are so much better."

It was the most his father had said to him in years, even before he had run away, and Eli wasn't sure if he should be taken aback or impressed that his father was capable of expressing emotions.

"I just—"

"You just think of yourself. Did you think maybe such a topic would be upsetting for your mother? For your sister? Did you think that despite you having forgotten and forsaken your family, that the family you left is still in mourning? Did you think that me not tearing my clothes and sobbing means I don't ache? That my heart is not screaming in pain?" Erel stood, picking up his plate. "You always thought of our minhag and our faith as a weakness, as a prison that kept you chained away from the life you wanted." He fixed Eli with a steely look. "But the mitzvot are not shackles that keep us chained; they are stairs that lift us up, that bring us closer to HaShem. They keep us balanced and keep our people alive." The fire slowly left his

60

belly, and his next words were softer. "They aren't always easy; things aren't always happy. We all grapple with pain and doubt. And ... when someone bucks against it, they can be fooled into thinking they are alone, that they are unloved. But it's not true." Erel shrugged. "There is nothing but love for them."

"I just want to know how my brother died. That's all," Eli said quietly.

"It doesn't matter," Erel said just as softly. "It doesn't matter at all how he died, only that he died, only that he's gone." Absentmindedly, he reached up and fiddled with a patch of torn fabric on his shirt, smoothing it like a worry stone. "I said he was my only son. But you know that isn't true. I am sad. Every day since you left, I am hurt. But you will never be anything but my son; you will never be ... treif, not to me." He took his plate to the sink and set it down. It looked like he would say more, but in the end, he let his silence fill the void and walked down the hall to his bedroom.

Neither Lilah or Ruth spoke. Seeing his father as human, someone who had actual feelings and expressed them, was frightening. It was so at odds with his normal stoicism. It created an uncomfortable weight over the table.

"Thank you for dinner," Eli mumbled as he stood. He scraped his plate into the trash and set it in the sink. "I'm going to turn in. I ... I'll go to the store tomorrow and buy a suit for the funeral ..." He stood there awkwardly for a moment. It felt like he was waiting for permission, but he knew what he needed was forgiveness. He also knew it wasn't coming. After another moment of awkwardly standing in silence, he turned and headed back into Dovev's room.

In Dovev's room, Eli pulled his backpack out and looked through his meager travel possessions. Computer, an old PSPgo, a novel, and Dovev's muscle mags. He sighed and pulled out the book. Cynthia had bought it for him to take along on his trip. She was a bookworm who was always trying to teach him the joys of reading. It was cute, a little hot in a "sexy librarian" sort of way, but it had never been his cup of tea. He would rather wait for the movie to come out or spend his time playing video games. But if he didn't at least try to read the book, it would hurt Cynthia's feelings. Now, in the dark room, needing to avoid his family until the morning, it seemed like as good a time as any to dive into whatever weird book Cynthia had recommended this time.

He looked at the book. It was a thin little affair with a naked woman on the cover—an upside-down triangle covering her pelvis—floating in front of an inverted church with an upside-down cross in front of her legs. All the upside-down imagery on the cover made it look like the woman, right side up, was actually upside down herself, creating a feeling of vertigo in the image.

Saint Sadist by Lucas Mangum. He hadn't heard of the author or the book before, but that wasn't shocking. Cynthia liked weird shit, always crawling through Facebook in niche book groups looking for her next fix. It was one reason Eli didn't want to read her books. They were fucked-up, every time. But she said this one was award-nominated, that it was as beautiful as it was terrifying. Not that Eli needed terrifying here, in the bed his brother died in, in the complex where someone was killed just this morning. But Eli pushed all that aside. Cynthia would ask him about the book when he got home, so to avoid any drama, he would at least try. He turned on the beside lamp, tucked himself in, and opened *Saint Sadist.*

Within minutes, Eli regretted the decision. The book was sickening and weird, to say the least. It was poetic and beautiful—even he could understand that—but it was intensely upsetting. He didn't want to read any more, but he just couldn't put it down. He wanted to know *why* Cynthia would want to read this, why it was award-nominated. So despite his desire to switch over to video games, he kept reading until he drifted off.

The lamp next to him flickered, the sporadic changing of light waking him from his light slumber. The book he had been reading lay next to his head, the thin spine cracked from resting open. Trying to operate with his eyes mostly closed so he didn't lose his sleepiness, Eli swatted at the lamp until he was able to find it and switch it off. He started to roll over when he caught the glimpse of the figure in the doorway of the room.

Adrenaline slammed through his body, and he sat up. It was her, the woman. She was ghostly white, seeming to glow in the darkness of the room. In the low light, she looked unnaturally beautiful, like the idea of an angel that stepped out of dreams and into the room with him. He could see the way her white slip clung to her slender curves, the way her long black hair hung about her, framing her face and shoulders in a cascade of darkness. Eli wanted a better look, or to wake up. He reached over towards the lamp.

Her hand grabbed his wrist. She was standing over him, looming.

"I don't—" he whispered, even in his dream afraid of waking the others. The memory of last night coursed through his body, giving birth to a painful erection. She seemed to know the effect she had on him. She slowly let go of his arm and reached down, her slender hand caressing his cock through the sheet. "I don't know your name." He knew it was a dream, but still, it felt so strange to be touched by someone he didn't know.

She met his eyes. The darkness made her gaze dark, seductive merely by its existence. She pulled her hand back from him so she could throw the sheet off of him. Without hesitation, she kneeled on the bed and kicked a leg over him so she was straddling him, facing his feet. She bent down, her hands gripping the waistband of his boxers and pulling them over his stiff cock. The cool air and her hot breath touching his skin as his erection was freed from the confines of his clothes pulled a gasp from him. He could still stop this. But in front of his face, her slip was riding up, exposing her round, perfect ass and her pussy, which glistened in the darkness of the room.

Her lips traveled up and down his dick, soft kisses that were driving him mad, before he felt her lips open and slide over the head of his penis. It was too much. If this was a dream, then dammit, he would enjoy it. He lifted his head and buried his face in her pussy, using his arms to pull her closer and squeeze her hips. He was rewarded as he felt her groan of pleasure around his throbbing dick in her mouth.

She tasted incredible, like someone had spiced a 9-volt battery, slightly metallic but with comforting notes. He wouldn't normally notice the flavor as he explored her with his tongue, licking and sucking on her clit, but it was so pleasant. And her tongue and mouth moving over him was driving him wild. It was all he could do to keep from bucking his hips and fucking her face—though considering this was a dream, he doubted she would have minded. He continued eating her out, wildly and with abandon, his only goal to help her get off before he came, and with her expert administrations, he knew he didn't have much time.

Eli could feel himself getting closer. "I'm going to—" he

started to say, to warn her, but she reacted by bobbing her head all the way down and pushing her hips back, forcing his face back to work.

As her lips hit the base of his shaft, Eli couldn't control himself. With a grunt, he came, an orgasm that felt like it would never end. He poured into her as she rode his face. He kept licking, sucking, and working on her, but he felt his consciousness fleeing, as though his ability to stay awake and perform had ejaculated out of his cock along with his cum. He faded, his eyes closing, the feeling of her weight on top of him disappearing as he drifted off.

TUESDAY

7

Eli woke up earlier than he wanted to, but he was starting to get used to the east coast time. His boxers were down around his thighs, and the lamp next to his head was still on. He groaned a little. He felt sore, like he had run a marathon. But, of course, he hadn't; he had apparently just jerked off in his sleep. But goddamn, what an incredible dream. He looked down at himself, examining the skin around his flaccid penis. There was no blood today. That was a relief. He lifted his ass to pull his boxers up and over his junk. He was sticky and still buzzing from the incredible orgasm from the dream.

Nothing a shower wouldn't fix. Eli pulled himself out of bed, the absence of blood making him almost giddy. He grabbed a change of clothes and headed to take a shower, almost skipping in postcoital euphoria. But as he grabbed the handle of the door, he remembered today was the day they would bury his brother. Eli stood there in the half-light of the room for a moment, trying to grapple with the shitty nature of his own psyche. His brother was dead, there was a murder in this very building, but all he could think about was the incredible dream-encounter he'd had last night. He needed to get his head right. Hopefully after the funeral, the cops would clear him and he could get back home.

His mood completely soured, he pushed through the hallway and into the bathroom. He didn't bother flipping the light switch, letting the little night light in the room be enough to get clean. He showered quickly in the dark, cursing the cold water in the pipes—one more reason to flee back to the relative warmth of the Californian December. He sighed and shut off the water, jumping out of the shower and drying quickly so he could get dressed before he caught his death of cold. The cold water had washed away all remnants of lust and excitement in his body. He flicked the switch on the wall, deciding he might as well get ready and go buy a cheap suit.

As he turned toward the mirror above the sink, he almost shrieked. There in the mirror where his reflection should be, Dovev stood. There was no mistaking his younger brother; the man looked just like their father minus some weight and years. Eli brought his breathing under his control. He must still be dreaming; that was the only real explanation.

"Dov ..." Eli whispered, reaching out to touch the mirror.

The image of his brother didn't respond, simply staring into Eli's soul with his deep brown eyes.

"Oh goddamn, Dov, I'm so sorry. I should have ... taken

you with me."

His brother didn't speak to answer him but slowly shook his head, his sorrow tangible even through the mirror. But as he shook his head, Eli realized there was someone else in the mirror. Just over the reflection's shoulder stood the incredibly beautiful face of the girl from the hallway. His nocturnal dream-lover. Her eyes in the light were large and dark, like pools of void; her lipstick smudged, giving her a messy but sensual appearance. The memory of the dream came back, making his body ache for her touch again. She looked away from him towards the door, then back to him, a slow smile spreading across her face, cruel but welcoming and full of promise.

A scream tore through the building, startling Eli. He turned towards the door as if he could see what was happening outside the bathroom through the flimsy door, then turned back towards the mirror. There was no one there but his reflection. A patch of dried blood covered his face from chin to just below his nose, having resisted the basic rinse he had done in the shower. Freaking out, he quickly bent down in the sink to scrub the red residue off his face.

What the hell? Why was he waking up covered in blood? And what was the connection to the hypersexual dreams? Was the cold air causing nosebleeds? It seemed the most rational explanation, but rational had less and less sway lately. He looked up, almost scared he would see his brother and that beautiful woman again, but only his face was there, rubbed raw from scrubbing.

He didn't have time to worry about the dreams and blood at the moment, though; the sounds of shouting and commotion floated through the thin walls of the apartment.

Eli got dressed quickly and headed out of the bathroom to make his way towards the foyer and door of the apartment. His parents were already there, as was Lilah. His mom looked scared, frightened of what they would find. His father, on the other hand, looked exhausted, like all of this was weighing on his heart in a way that was physically killing him, and maybe it was. Lilah had a strange look on her face. She looked resolute. Eli chalked it up to trying to put on a brave face.

"Do you know what that scream was?" Eli asked as he joined them.

"How would we know?" Erel asked. "We are in here with you."

Eli rolled his eyes. "Just seeing if someone had heard anything." He reached past them and pushed the front door of the apartment open. There was a large throng of people down the hallway, gathered outside 110a. An older woman, probably his mother's age, stood at the center of the throng, her clothes soaked in gore.

"Jesus!" Eli yelped as he took in the sight of the woman, drawing several scowls, but Eli wasn't paying attention to anyone but the woman and the door. He didn't know what possessed him as he pushed his way through the crowd and into the woman's apartment, but he was driven to see—like passing a bad wreck on the side of the road, he had to crane his neck to see what had happened. He regretted this need as soon as he entered the apartment.

In 109b, the man had been slaughtered in his bed, ripped apart with unholy fury where he lay. There was no telling where this man had been killed in here. He was everywhere. Pieces of flesh and body parts had been flung across the apartment. An arm lay in several pieces on the dining room table, each finger on the hand broken and twisted into unnatural positions. The fridge was open, and he could see the man's head, minus his jaw, sitting in a pool of tacky blood. One eye was missing, with what looked disturbingly like teeth marks around the empty socket. The other was bloodshot and bulged from the socket. The smell of copper was overpowering, mixed with the rotten stench of feces that wafted from the pile of torn and shredded intestines oozing over the side of the sofa. He stepped further in, doing his best to avoid the places where scraps of flesh had landed.

The level of savagery was incredible. He would suspect a bear if there were any signs of destruction other than the man's corpse. But all the furniture seemed undamaged, as though a tornado of blades had come into the home, ripped apart a single old man, and then departed, leaving all else untouched. It was a surreal and nightmarish scene. Every cell in his body was screaming at him to leave, to pack up his meager belongings and fuck off back to California. He took a step forward, deeper into the room. Something clattered across the tile as he kicked it. Glancing down, he saw several teeth. They looked too small to have come from the jawless head in the fridge, like they had been wrenched out of children. The thought made Eli's stomach turn.

"What are you doing?!" someone shouted from behind him.

Eli turned, feeling as though he were in a daze—everything felt far away, dreamlike; his head was swimming. "I—"

"You can't just go in—get out!" The man was shouting at him from the doorway.

Eli took a step forward towards the door and lost his balance. He fell towards the ground but was caught before he hit by the shouting young Chassid.

"What is wrong with you?" he said, less concerned with Eli's well-being than with his lack of decorum. He dragged Eli back into the hall. "That is a crime scene. You can't just go in there."

"I just …" Eli tried to think straight, but it felt like every word he tried to grasp flitted away before he could speak. "I just wanted to help."

"You don't help by interfering." He propped Eli up against

the wall next to the open door. "Erel, this is your son, yes? You should control him better."

"Who else's son should he be?" Erel asked as he walked up. "Should I put him on a leash? He has never listened to me. But he is just worried; he meant no harm."

They continued to argue politely, but Eli couldn't focus. Across the hall, he saw her. She wasn't panicking or gossiping with the others, and despite the white slip clinging to her slender curves, leaving painful little to the imagination, no one seemed to notice her. Eli blinked slowly. Why was no one freaking out that a woman was being immodest next to a murder scene? Was he going insane? He reached out a hand towards the woman. She shook her head with a smile and lifted a finger to her lips. Maintaining eye contact, she slowly licked the digit from her knuckle to the top before giving her nail a kiss.

The vertigo hit him like a truck. His vision whirled around the hallway. In an attempt to escape the dizziness, he closed his eyes. In the darkness of his own head, the world around him and the sound of the crowd slipped away, along with his consciousness.

Eli sat up with a start. He was in his brother's room, a cold rag on his head. At the foot of the bed, his mother sat. Her back was to him, but he could see she was knitting. Or crocheting. He didn't know the difference, only that once she was done, someone would have a new sweater or scarf.

"What happened?" he asked.

"You fainted," she answered. "Are you okay now?"

"I don't know." Eli watched her. She didn't turn to face him as they spoke, her focus remaining on her work. It reminded him of when he was little. She always seemed so focused, like the whole world was in her hook and yarn. When he was a kid, he likened her to HaShem, the respectful name for God. Aware of everything but focused on the work of building creation. It was comforting to him then, imaging god as a mother who was knitting together the world, making it cozy and warm ... loving. It was a damn nicer mental picture than god as the angry dismissive father. Maybe if he had been able to hold on to god as "Ima," he would never have left.

"I'm sorry," he said finally.

"For what?" she asked him. "I don't think you intended to faint, though I think you need to work on your instincts. Rushing into a crime scene—what if the killer had still been there? You should be more careful."

"Yeah ..." he said. He watched her shoulders moving slowly as she worked in the low light of the room. "Mom, Ima ..."

She paused in her work, setting the knitting in her lap. Her shoulder's shook, and the sound of quiet sobs, muffled behind her hands, was the only sound in the room. Eli looked down, staring at his hands, unsure what to say, deeply uncomfortable with her tears. It struck him that this wasn't anything new. How often had his mother sat in the dark crying … because of him? And now, here she was again, in her dead son's room, with the son she probably considered dead. He couldn't imagine how empty, how lonely she felt.

Being here, being around her and Lilah, it made them human, made them more than the caricatures he had turned them into in his head. In his memory, his mother was a shadow, a ghost haunting the house under the kaiju-esque presence of his father. Confronted here with the truth, that his mother was not an extension of his dad but rather a flesh and blood person, a human in her own right, with her own story, and, most of all, her own hurt—it was almost too much for him to process.

"I can't imagine how hurt, how scared you must be," he finally said. His words sounded like shouts in the quiet of the room. "I'm so sorry about Dov—"

"I imagined you coming home so many times, Elijah. I thought about it every single day. Every single hour. You're my son, my first son. And I thought about how we would welcome you, how we would … do whatever it took to make sure you knew that you were … that you were home." Her voice shook with raw emotion.

"Dovev always tried to convince me that it wouldn't happen, that you didn't think about us," she continued. "But I always thought about how the Amish do that ritual Rumspinga, how they go and experience the world and then they come back to their home and they rejoin the community, choosing to serve Adoynoi and their community above themselves. And maybe it was foolish, maybe it was greedy of me. But a mother is allowed to be greedy, isn't she? A mother is allowed to hold on to hope, even if it is foolish."

"I couldn't … I don't want to live this life," Eli said, trying to muster up the righteous anger, but everything his family was saying to him struck him like a physical blow. The knowledge that he had hurt them more deeply and more completely than he had ever been hurt opened an ache deep within his soul.

"Even if you can't rejoin the Chassidic community, even if you abandoned HaShem and religion, I prayed you would come back to us, that our love, our family was more important than your anger."

"How could I when religion is all that was here."

"You truly think that I wouldn't have—no, that I don't still love you? I love you no matter who you are, I loved you from the minute you were born, and there is nothing in HaShem's entire creation that could change that. But I know you don't feel this way, that to you, this is an onus, that it is a burden you must sit through before you can escape again. I had … I hoped that coming back, that I would be able to reclaim one of my sons. That I could fill the emptiness. But the anger you hold on to, Elijah, the anger you hold on to is killing you and leaves me with no sons at all."

"I'm sorry," Eli said. He felt the hollow of his chest expand as if it were a chasm in the earth opening to swallow him. He had never considered that he could still have any sort of relationship with any part of his family if he wasn't going to be a part of the religious community. He had never even entertained the possibility, and he had certainly never given them the chance. "I ... missed you," he finally said, and was surprised to find that it was true.

"I ... I would like to try to have a relationship," he said, but felt less sure about that. Maybe he was only saying that because of how emotional he felt in that moment; maybe when he got back to California, he would go back to his sequestered life away from his past. But in that moment, he would have done anything to mend the hurt between himself and his mother.

"I would too, Elijah," she said, rising. "You slept for a while. The police have already come and gone. But the Rebbe has called a specialist to help." She gathered her yarn and met his eyes, hers red-rimmed and puffy. Even in the low light, it was easy to see the emotional toll the loss of one son and the reappearance of the other had taken on her. "If you want to avoid overly religious experiences, you don't need to come out and see him."

He realized she was attempting to show him she could respect his lack of religion, that she could meet him halfway.

He felt obligated to do the same. "No, I'll … I want to know what is going on. I would like to see him." Eli paused. "Oh crap, how long have I been out? I need to go buy a suit for Dov's funeral!"

"You should just wear one of Dov's suits," his mother offered.

"Isn't that a little morbid? And isn't there a—I don't know, isn't there some superstition that wearing his clothes could confuse the angel of death? Make them take me too?" Eli smirked; he remembered some of the pageantry and folklore.

Ruth shook her head before turning to leave the room. "Hand-me-downs and borrowing clothes, that's just the way things are, Elijah. Just … if you insist, just hurry. You only have a few hours before the funeral."

"Yes, Ima," Eli replied, watching her walk out.

After she was gone, he looked around the small room, opening the door to Dov's closet to look for a suit to wear, but the truth was he didn't want to wear his brother's clothes. He didn't believe the angel of death would come and take him; he didn't believe in stuff like that. Although, he was still shaken by the visage of his brother and the woman in the mirror. The woman. Holy shit, was he insane? He saw her in the hallway just before passing out. Maybe he had a brain tumor or something that was causing him to hallucinate.

Or maybe it was stress—being back here, his brother's

death, and confronting emotions and memories he had so long repressed was causing him to crack. Eli closed Dov's closet. No, getting out of here for even a few hours would be great. It would give him a chance to breathe, to reset. He grabbed his wallet and phone and headed out.

8

As Eli approached the doors to the apartment building, he saw a group of men standing near the door. There was an old, squat Chassid standing there speaking.

The man was speaking in Yiddish. He spoke softly, with the sort of patience you develop from dealing with bone-headed fundamentalists your entire life, not that he looked any better. The other men muttered, arguing back and forth. Eli assumed this must be the specialist his mom had mentioned. He approached quietly to see if he could overhear, interested in determining what sort of specialist he was, if nothing else. Unfortunately, *all* of them were speaking in Yiddish. Eli could catch a word here or there but, for the most part, was entirely lost.

"I'm sorry, what's going on?" he asked when there was a small break in the clamor.

"Ah, I was just telling your ..." The man looked at Eli, a look of confusion crossing his face. "I'm sorry, who are you?"

"Eli, er, Elijah Rosenbaum. My family lives here. I came in for—"

"For the funeral. I am sorry for your loss. Erel tells me Dov was a good man. My name is Reb Nathan Schulman. It is nice to meet you." He offered his hand, which Eli took in a brief shake. "Anyway, I was just telling your neighbors that I noticed the Mezuzah on the outside entry as well as on three of the doors have been damaged."

"Okay, is that … is that important?" Eli asked, ignoring the dirty looks he was getting from the other men—at least this Nathan didn't seem to resent him.

"Eh, I think so, yes. All details are important; it is just a matter of if they are pertinent at the moment. But I believe that these tragedies are caused by something … not human."

Eli felt his blood run cold, which pissed him off. He was no child that believed in monsters. He didn't even believe in god, so what was a dumb ghost story other than something to get in the way of finding the actual answers.

"I see," he said. He wanted to discount the man, call him just another deluded religious fanatic. But the vision of his brother and the girl came back to his mind, as well as old legends. And the teeth. He had seen teeth at both murder scenes. "Uh … you mean like a dybbuk?" he asked.

"A dybbuk? No, a dybbuk would not be—" He paused, peering at Eli with an intense curiosity that made Eli uncomfortable. "You've seen something." It was not a question.

"I don't know. I was—I was just very tired," Eli stammered.

Nathan turned back to the assembled men and said something in Yiddish before turning back to Eli. "Show me

81

where?"

Eli thought about shrugging him off, saying he had to go get a suit, go prepare, but now he couldn't shake the feeling that maybe he had seen something, that maybe there was something going on. He led Reb Schulman through the complex to his parents' door. The dour man reached up and unfastened the mezuzah, pulling it open and tapping it until a small pile of ashes and the remnants of a scorched scroll fell into his palm. "I doubt that is kosher," he said softly.

Eli shrugged. He didn't know what the significance of any of this was, but he knew that inside the mezuzah should be a whole, undamaged scroll with some prayer or mitzvot written on it. "So what does that mean?"

"A mezuzah's purpose is three-fold. The first use is to tell the world and other Jews that this home is a safe place for Jews. It broadcasts that you are a member of the tribe and all that entails. The second is to keep us mindful of the mitzvot. That it is not just out there in the open we must be good and righteous, but within our homes as well. Conversely, it reminds us that as we do step out, we take our identity with us, representing the Jewish people to the world as a whole." It was obvious Schulman enjoyed lecturing. "Finally, and maybe most esoterically, the mezuzah acts as a talisman of protection. It rebuffs spirits and sheydim. Or it is supposed to. So yes, seeing it destroyed in such a manner is very troubling."

82

Instead of answering, he just opened the door and led Schulman into the apartment. His mother and sister started at his sudden return with the Rebbe in tow. "Uh, I just ... need to show ..." Eli trailed off and walked to the bathroom.

"This morning, right before we found out about ... what had happened, I saw my brother and—" Eli stopped himself. "My brother in this mirror."

"Your brother has yet to be buried. It is possible he might be here, his nefesh, waiting to be buried so he may return to the cycle of *gilgul*."

"What is gilgul?" Eli asked.

"For another time," Schulman said.

"Well, I just thought between that and the teeth—"

"Teeth?" Schulman interrupted.

"In both apartments, I saw teeth ... and in the first, there was this box, covered in wax and seals. I think it might have been a dybbuk box ..." Eli trailed off, feeling absolutely ridiculous. He didn't know shit about any of this other than what he had seen in random horror movies or read on Reddit. He hoped Schulman wouldn't laugh at him, but part of him hoped he did. He wanted to hear that all this supernatural bullshit was just that, bullshit. That there was a human killer on the loose—while that didn't make him safe, it meant a person who could be caught. He didn't like the intense and fearful look on the man's face.

"There's no such thing as a Dybbuk box, young man.

Dybbukim do not haunt objects or get trapped in boxes. But a box of teeth is something else entirely, something that I would rather not believe is unleashed here." Schulman paused. "When you said you saw your brother, you were about to say something else that you saw. What was it?" His dark eyes burned into Eli.

"I, uh, I saw a woman. A young woman. In the mirror," Eli admitted.

"What?" gasped Lilah.

"A woman?" Erel asked from the hall.

"Uh … yeah, a woman. I've seen here outside too, in the hall, around the complex, near the doors of … Look, I just saw her, okay?"

"Have you seen her anywhere else?" Schulman asked.

Eli turned red, thinking of his vivid dreams. "No," he answered.

"Elijah, have you seen her in your dreams? Have you … coupled with her in your dreams?"

"Don't ask him that!" Ruth cried.

"That's inappropriate, Rebbe," Erel chided.

Lilah looked pale, horrified, as though the entire concept of a ghostly woman appearing to Eli was the nightmare instead of what had been done to those poor men.

Eli's mouth hung open, his eyes darting between the prying little rabbi and his family. "I don't—"

"No lies!" the rabbi snapped at him. "This is very important.

I need to know, have you spilled your seed while dreaming of this woman?"

"Jesus!" Eli said, throwing his hands up. "What the fuck are you asking me?"

"Your defensiveness is answer enough," Schulman said. "I have to go."

"Go?" Erel asked. "Why—"

"I don't have what I need to face down what has latched on to your son. I need supplies. I should call—" A look of brief sadness crossed his features. "I need to get assistance. I apologize, but there is no time to—"

Just then, there was a loud bang as someone knocked on the door to the apartment.

"Police! Open up!"

All five of them froze, staring in the direction of the door.

"We have a warrant for Elijah Rosenbaum."

"What? What did you say to them? Why are they here for me?!" Eli asked, suddenly panicked.

"I said nothing!" Erel snapped at him as he moved towards the door to let the police in.

"Wait!" Schulman snapped. "He cannot leave the building."

"Rebbe, I am not going to fight with the police. They'll take Eli and discover he had nothing to do with this. If we try to hide him or he runs, it will be as good as an admission of guilt. They will throw him away or execute him. Do not ask me to lose two sons this week."

Schulman looked like he was going to try to stop Erel, but Eli's old man was already at the door, opening it for the police. Eli came around the corner. He didn't agree with his dad. He had watched the BLM riots on TV, and all of his friends involved in law had told him to never, under *any* circumstances, talk to the cops. But here they were. He could see that young asshole Lt. Spence—he had a cruel grin on his face.

"Elijah Rosenbaum, you are under arrest for the murder of Yosef Lev and Alexander Gamberg."

Eli stared numbly at them as they entered his parents' home and pushed him roughly against the wall, wrenching his arms behind his back and cuffing him. He was dimly aware they were reading his rights, but at the same time, he could hear Schulman arguing with them, begging them not to remove Eli from the building. He didn't know why the man was so agitated. Wouldn't getting him out of the building mean he was out of danger?

They started dragging Eli out of the apartment, shoving him towards the front of the building. Eli's family and Schulman followed closely after them, Schulman speaking the entire time, growing more and more frantic.

"Please, you must understand, this thing will not allow him to leave. It is not concerned with morality, with secrecy, it will—"

"Look, old man," Lt. Spence suddenly snapped, whirling on the elderly rabbi. "If you don't stop trying to get in our way, I'm going to fucking cuff you too and bring you in for obstruction. I don't know what the fuck you're babbling about, but nothing is going to stop us from bringing in this bloodthirsty piece of shit."

"Hey!" Eli protested.

"Shut your mouth. You make me sick," Spence spat.

"What happened to innocent until proven otherwise?" Eli snapped.

Spence rewarded the question with a punch to the temple, dropping Eli to his knees. His wrist screamed in agony as the other cop wrenched him back to his feet and started force-marching him towards the door again.

"Do not hit my son," Erel roared, but shrunk back as Spence turned his cruel eyes on him. The look nearly screamed that all he needed was an excuse to start beating any of the Jews around him. He didn't need to; he wanted to.

"Please, I am begging you—" Schulman continued as they reached the entry to the building.

As Spence reached for the handle, the door to the nearest apartment opened. There she stood, the woman in white. Eli's head spun as he met her dark eyes. Even in this terrible moment of duress, he was stunned by her beauty. "She is real," he muttered as the cops turned to look at her.

"Ma'am, return insi—" Spence began, but before he could finish, the woman was gone. "What?" he said, confused by her disappearance.

"FUCK!" the other cop cried out.

Eli turned his head just in time to see that she had somehow gotten behind Lt. Spence. Schulman and his family were backtracking, stumbling to get away from the girl. Only Lilah stood still, gaping at the figure.

The woman met Eli's eyes, a glimmer of lust and playful mischief there, but as she turned her gaze back to Spence, all playfulness and warmth fled her visage. She reached out and grabbed him by the throat. Blood welled up as her nails punctured his flesh, his panicked gurgling filling the hall.

"Drop him!" the other cop screamed, releasing Eli—who fell to the floor—in order to pull his gun and aim it at the woman. "You fucking drop him right this second, or so fucking help me, I'll shoot you in the goddamn face."

The woman, who had been calmly studying Spence's face as he choked on his own blood, turned her gaze slowly to the other cop. Her lips twitched in a sardonic smile. She did not release Spence, instead raising her other hand to his chest to leverage her grip.

"I said drop him!" The man's voice was becoming a shrill scream of primal fear.

She shook her head and turned her eyes back to Lt. Spence.

His face was white; he still sputtered. His hands flailed, hitting her arms and head, doing anything he could to try to break her grip, but nothing he did had any effect, and it was obvious he was growing weaker by the second. She shook her head again and, with startling nonchalance, closed her fist and tore his throat out. His lifeless body fell to the ground, his esophagus, windpipe, and tongue flopping in her clenched hand. She smiled wide as she tossed the bloody meat to the ground.

The hall filled with the sound of gunshots as the second cop, the only one still standing, unloaded his magazine into the woman. Her body jerked and spasmed as each bullet tore through her, leaving gaping entry wounds. But she did not fall; she did not even retreat a step.

The gun clicked as he continued to pull the trigger. Before he could reach for his belt, she was on him. As she moved, her wounds closed. Bullets pushed out of torn flesh, which knitted itself whole as it expelled the projectiles.

Her thumbs found his eye sockets and plunged deep. With her handhold on his skull, she clambered up his body and perched on his shoulders. She was feral, her movements inhuman, but still every inch of her, every move she made dripped with attraction for Eli. He couldn't tear his eyes away from her. She was real. Had they really ...?

His thoughts were interrupted as she suddenly stood upright on the officer's shoulders. Her thumbs still buried in his eye

89

sockets, the force tore the top of his skull off, showering the area with cranial meat and blood. The man's screams lost their definition as his brain died. What had started as a shrill fear-fueled shriek tapered off into a low unintelligible moan as he toppled backwards and slumped dead against the wall.

Eli felt himself being pulled off the ground and yanked backward.

"Run, boy! Run!" Schulman was shouting at him.

Eli let himself be led, even as he watched the woman clamber off the corpse and turn towards him. Her eyes locked with his, and she offered him a slow, delicious smile that promised everything he had ever wanted. She did not pursue as Eli was dragged through a doorway, the door slammed shut and locked as soon as he was through.

9

Cacophony.

There was no other word that could describe the sheer wall of noise being created by the handful that had escaped into the apartment. The Rosenbaums, Schulman, and a few Chassidim who had been in the hall when the thing had attacked, all huddled in the foyer of the apartment. Nothing more than a flimsy particle board door separated them from the creature that had just murdered two armed policemen without hesitation. A creature that had survived an entire magazine worth of bullets being emptied into it. Her. Eli's brain tried to wrap around the concept that there was something supernatural in the building. But with the noise, fear, and arousal swirling around him, it was like trying to grasp at strands of straw thrown into a hurricane.

"What was that?" Erel's voice rose above the noise.

Slowly, the arguing and weeping settled down, and all eyes turned towards the elderly Rabbi Schulman.

"That was what I was afraid of. Do you know how rare it is? Hmm? To see something like that, to come face to face with true evil? That was one of the Lillim, a daughter of Lillith from the time of Adam, an ancient creature that sustains herself on the blood and semen of human men."

"A demon, Rabbi?" Erel said skeptically. "You think it not more reasonable that it is some ill woma—"

"A mentally ill woman could not do what she did," another voice argued.

"But a demon? Really?"

"I did not say it was a demon. It is … not Sheyd. It is much more powerful and much more dangerous," Schulman said. He looked at Eli. "Did you bring her here?"

It took a moment for Eli to realize what the old man was insinuating. He realized all eyes in the room were on him. He turned slowly, looking at the huddled mass of terrified Chassidim; only his sister, Lilah, avoided his eyes. "What? How would I have done that?" Eli struggled to rise, his hands still cuffed behind his back. Erel helped him stand.

"She's latched on to you, boy. Were you having dreams about her before you came here?" Schulman pressed.

"No," Eli said. "I never saw her before coming here. I saw her when I first came in. She was standing in the door of … 109b …."

That sent the group muttering again. As they muttered, Lilah moved behind him, and he felt her messing with the handcuffs. A moment later, they fell open. Eli brought his hands in front of him and rubbed his wrists, turning to give Lilah a confused look. She held up a hairpin and shrugged. He wanted to ask her where the hell she had learned to pick a lock, let alone a handcuff's lock, but before that, he needed to address the fact that he was being accused of bringing in a fucking demon.

"How do you mean she's latched on to me? None of this is my fault. I wouldn't even be here if not for my brother, and he died before I came. I came here because he died, so I couldn't be at fault for that." Eli hated weaponizing his brother's death, but he liked being blamed even less.

"You've been dreaming about her, erotic dreams, am I right? And when you see her in the flesh, you feel weak, right?" Schulman pressed.

Eli turned red at his words. He could feel his shame and embarrassment burning in his ears.

"Stop it," Ruth suddenly said. "That creature, that murderer is on the other side of this door, and you sit here accusing Elijah of this horrible thing. He had nothing to do with it. If she is using him, it is not his choice, or his fault."

As if on cue, something slammed into the door leading to the hallway. Everyone grew silent and shrunk away from the door, crowding into the living room. They all stayed there huddled for several minutes, waiting for the woman to break through and continue the slaughter.

"But if he remained faithful, if he said his blessings—" Erel said softly.

"But he doesn't, and there is an entire world of goyim out there that do not, and they are not held prisoner by some demon.

Not another word on whose fault the creature is. If you want to be useful ..."—she glared daggers at all the men—"then discover how we can escape with our lives."

There was a long silence. No one wanted to confront the mother.

Finally, Schulman nodded. "You are right, of course, Mrs. Rosenbaum. Listen, everyone. It is vitally important than no one try to remove Elijah Rosenbaum from the premises. I will go and find help."

"What help can you find for a demon? You're the specialist, aren't you?" Erel asked.

"Yes," Schulman said with a sigh. "But I am no Baal Shem. I can't simply pray such a thing away. But that doesn't mean we are without hope." He rose and looked around the small apartment they had all rushed into. "Is there a back door? Someway to get out of here?"

"No, no door," Erel said, standing slowly. "But there are windows connected to the fire escape. We could use that."

"Not we, Mr. Rosenbaum, me. The more people that try to escape, the more likely she is to intervene. Until I know more, we must mitigate that risk. But yes, that works. I will go and get help, the kind of help that can really make a difference. I can hold her off for a while, but I cannot banish her on my own."

"This is impossible. Demons aren't real," Eli muttered, looking around at the faces of the Chassidim around him.

None of them would meet his eyes. They hid their shame at agreeing with him, a facade of faith and belief. But it was one thing to believe in your heart; it was another thing entirely to be confronted with the nightmarish truth of monsters. Questions of why bad things happen and debates on the reason for childhood cancer were all fine and good with nebulous beliefs. He knew they were struggling with their beliefs because he was now struggling with his disbeliefs.

Schulman looked around the room; the weary frown on his face spoke volumes. He was not struggling the way everyone else in the room was. He had known these things were real. He had obviously seen concrete proof before, and he had seen people struggling. He nodded. "I know that is a comfort that you had allowed yourself, Elijah. It is what keeps us sane, what keeps us whole and capable, for it is written in *Berachot*: *If the eye had the power to see them, no creature could endure the demons. They are more numerous than we are and they surround us like the ridge around a field.* So I understand your hesitation to believe. But that luxury is beyond you now, beyond all of us." He took another look around and nodded to Erel. "Can you show me where the window with the fire escape is?"

Erel rose. So did everyone else. Being alone felt terrifying; maybe there could be strength in numbers—never mind the fact that the creature had murdered two armed policemen in a

95

hallway filled with people. Safety was an illusion, but it was the only comfort they could grasp on to. As a herd, they shuffled through the living room to the kitchen, where there was a large window leading to a small, rickety ladder down to the ground outside.

Schulman nodded and turned to face the gathering behind him. "Just stay in here, stay calm, do not panic, and do not try to leave. So long as you do these things, I believe she will bide her time. Then I will return with help." He smiled reassuringly and turned to grab the window and pull it open.

No sooner had his hands landed on the window sill than the thin, pale, and blood-drenched hand of the woman—the *lillim*—shot out of the shadows and gripped his wrist with enough strength to crush the bones to dust. Schulman screamed in pain and shock, struggling against her. She stepped out of the shadows, head cocked to one side, regarding the terrified group before her. She lifted her arm, pulling Schulman off his feet, dangling by the stretching skin of his now boneless wrist. Wordlessly, she clucked her tongue in disapproval.

"Atah gabor l'ola—" Schulman whimpered out the beginnings of a prayer, but before he could even get the third word out, she released his arm. As he fell, she caught his head in her other hand and slammed it into the wall next to the window. The thin wall crumpled like paper, and she dragged his head through the crumbling drywall, leaving bits of scalp and hair along the way, until she reached a stud. There, she slammed his skull into the thick wooden beam again and again, until all that was left was a pulverized mess of flesh and bone, brains and lacerated tongue dripping from between her fingers. She left his body there, slumped and half buried in the debris of the wall, and turned towards the terrified onlookers.

The group had watched in spellbound terror as she murdered the old man, no one daring to even breathe, but her look broke the spell, and they scrambled over each other in an attempt to flee. Eli was carried in the wave of people, trying to keep his footing as he was swept towards the door. As they reached the door, the man in the front, Eli didn't know his name, flung it open, only to be greeted by a wall of darkness that certainly shouldn't have been there. Her laughter rang out from the kitchen—booming, sonorous—and it made Eli ache with a need to return to her. The mob was already moving, though, pushing them out into the darkness of the hallway. Lilah, at the back of the crowd, closed the door behind her, cutting off the sound of the laughter and the only source of light, plunging them into a deep, black void.

Eli reached into his pocket and pulled out his phone, pushing the flashlight button to give them some light. Something was deeply wrong. All around them were brick walls, completely at odds with the dilapidated wallpaper that should have surrounded them. Instead of a straight shot to the front door leading out of the building, the brick hall stretched in three directions, a maze that should not exist.

One of the men that Eli didn't know fell to his knees, weeping and praying with fervor. Erel, for his part, looked angry, as though he could be stern at the sudden wrongness of the universe and force it to right itself. He looked back at the door they had just exited from and then to either direction.

Eli brought the phone up, hoping he could call the cops, but the little icon at the top of the phone informed him he had no signal, no way to call out. No way to call for help. He closed his eyes, dropping his hands to his side, feeling utterly defeated. At that moment, he wished he had just ignored that call, let it go to voicemail. He could have gone back to California and then sent flowers from an online store. No one would have questioned it; no one would have cared. Instead, he had come back; against every instinct in every fiber of his being, he had come back. Maybe he was insane. Maybe coming back home had been the first sign of some new mental illness and break with reality.

"Elijah ... shine your light down the hallway," Erel ordered, the suddenness of the words catching Eli off guard.

Even during all of this, with everything that had just happened in the last few minutes, his first instinct was to tell his father to shove it up his ass. But he swallowed the vitriol he felt—it had no purpose, no use—and did as he was told. He shined the light to the left, and then the right, and then straight ahead. In all three directions, the brick walls continued as though they would go on for eternity. They stood in silence for several minutes before Eli started walking.

"Where are you going?" Lilah asked, echoing what everyone else was wondering.

"We can't stay here," Eli responded, turning. "I don't know what's going on. I ... I think ... it's like Salem, right, there must be mold in the walls, or something in the water ..."

"Salem?" Erel asked, shaking his head. "What are you talking about?"

"Oh my god, this is why I left. You don't know—"

"Elijah!" His mother's voice cracked like a whip. "This is not the time."

Eli looked down, mollified. She was right; they were all going insane, people were dead, and here he was trying to pick fights with an old, scared man. "The Salem witch trials. It's a famous thing in American history. Historians think that maybe everyone was tripping on ergot. It's a fungus that grows on wheat. Mass hallucination that led to a lot of innocent people dying. They thought everyone was a witch." He shrugged. "I don't have another explanation for all of this."

"The explanation?" Erel asked. "The explanation for a demon that you have been ... intimate with these last few nights?"

"Jesus, Aba." Eli rubbed his eyes with his free hand. "Can

we just …" He gestured towards the path he had started down. "Let's go. There has to be an end to this. Either we're tripping balls and we'll come down and see what's real, right, *or* you're right, and it's a demon fucking with us. Either way, waiting here for her to come out the apartment and kill someone else just doesn't really seem like a good fucking idea." He stood there for a moment, looking over the group, seeing if anyone else had a better idea. When no one objected, he turned and continued down the hallway.

They walked for hours.

Every so often, Eli would check the phone battery, watching as the flashlight function slowly ate into it. He knew it wouldn't last much longer; he was already down to 10%. He had also been checking the signal strength every few minutes. Nothing.

"What are you doing?" Lilah asked, stepping up beside Eli as he led the way.

"Trying to figure out what we're going to do. I feel like whatever is going on should have worn off by now. But we're still here …" He gestured to the brick walls on either side of them.

"Maybe it isn't wheat mold," she said lightly. "Maybe Aba and the Rebbe were right."

"No. That's not … Shit, Lilah, if demons were real and attacked people, don't you think that people would know that?

Don't you think there would be even a sliver of proof somewhere in the world?"

"Only if there were survivors," she whispered. She sounded angry. He couldn't blame her. Her entire life had been upended; she had to be scared and confused. He sure as hell was.

"We're going to survive, Lilah. It's going to be okay. And honestly, I know you wouldn't know this, but sometimes a bad trip can mess with your sense of time, like a few moments can feel like years. For all we know, it's only been a minute since we left that apartment." He paused, staring ahead.

"What is it?" Lilah whispered, suddenly afraid he had seen the woman ahead.

"Look, a doorway!" Eli hissed.

Sure enough, just at the end of the flashlight's reach, they could see a door recessed into the brick wall on the right. He rushed forward and grabbed the handle. Part of him was terrified he would open the door and find they had gone in a big circle, that he would find the corpse of Schulman. He stood there with his hand on the door for several seconds, waiting for the rest of their group to catch up. With everyone around him, he took a deep breath and tried the handle. The door swung inward, revealing the interior of an apartment.

For a moment, Eli was sure this was the same apartment they had fled earlier that day, but Erel pushed past him. "This is our home," he said gruffly, looking back at everyone. "This is my apartment."

Eli breathed a sigh of relief as Erel flipped the switch next to the door and the foyer lights flickered on, revealing old pictures of his family along the wall. He turned off his phone's flashlight and shoved it in his pocket. The group filed into the small home, and Erel locked the door behind them.

"How do we know this place is safer than the last apartment?" one man asked.

Eli looked at him, finally taking in the three members of their group who were not his immediate family. They were faceless to him, Chassidim who could have been anyone at all. To him, they all looked alike. But now they had been through so much, it seemed cruel to label them as incidental.

"We don't, Yitzak," Ruth said. "But we also don't know that the hallway was any safer either. Here, we at least have light, and cushions, and food." She pushed past the men and headed toward the kitchen. "Lilah, help me prepare something? Erel, get out some blankets and pillows for everyone."

Lilah frowned but finally followed her mother into the other room.

Eli thought it was weird how his parents seemingly fell into almost normal behavior the moment they were back in their home, but on the other hand, his stomach was painfully empty and he was exhausted, and was sure the others were too, so didn't say shit. After a few minutes, his parents reappeared with food and bedding. They all ate in silence, the fear and uncertainty robbing them all of their voices.

After dinner, everyone shuffled around the living room, finding places to sleep on the couch, on the recliner, even on the floor. Even though the Rosenbaums all had their own beds, their own rooms, no one wanted to be alone. The men whispered their prayers together. Eli wondered if they were performing the Mourner's Kaddish for those who had died, but traditionally, you had to have a group of ten men. Were they so stuck in their ways that they couldn't even mourn without fulfilling worthless commandments?

Finally, everyone settled. Ruth lit a few larger candles, something to keep the darkness at bay while keeping it dim enough to rest.

Lilah looked over at him and offered him a weak smile. "Erev tov, Eli."

He met her eyes. Maybe when they woke, this all would have passed, he would come to and find it had all been a horrible nightmare. He didn't know if he believed that, but it was all he could hope for at this point. "Goodnight, Lilah," he answered and curled into a ball next to the TV to try to fall asleep.

WEDNESDAY

10

Eli rolled over, unable to sleep. Too much blood, too much death, and the sudden realization there was more on this earth than he had ever dared believed. He was trying desperately to believe this was all some sort of terrible mass hallucination, but as the night wore on, it was getting harder and harder to hold on to that thought. Before this week, he had never believed in anything more supernatural than luck ... now, he had watched some sort of ancient Jewish demon tear apart Schulman and two police officers.

"For you."

The voice was in his ear, soft but startling. Eli turned to look over his shoulder, expecting to see Lilah or his mom, but instead, it was *her*. He scrambled away with a shout. He looked around wildly, assuming his sudden shouting would wake someone up, but no one moved. She was crouched there, where he had been laying, her dark eyes locked on to him. The intensity in her gaze made his head swim, his heart hurt, his loins ache. She slowly stood, smoothing her white slip across her body.

"Your aba was wrong, you know," she said. Her words were a sultry whisper that slinked across the air between them and caressed his ears. "They would not have cleared you. It isn't what they do. They wanted a scapegoat; they wanted someone for … *Azazel*." She said the word with such disdain that he found himself hating Azazel too, whatever the fuck that was.

"You're a killer. You killed them," he croaked, his voice coming out in a dry rasp. He looked around for something to arm himself with, anything he could use to defend himself from the monster who watched him. Why was no one waking up?

"Oh, all things are killers. It's a matter of degree, Eli."

The use of his name nearly pulled a gasp from him. Her voice was the perfect accompaniment to her physical presence. Every inch of her body and demeanor screamed at him to be taken.

"How many cockroaches have you stepped on? How many meals of meat have you devoured? It's all degrees, Eli." She took a step toward him. He tried to retreat further, but he found himself backed into a wall. She did not pause in her advance.

"The cops were just roaches to you," he said, desperate to keep her talking and not killing, the vision of what she had done to them swimming in his mind.

"Less than that," she agreed as she lowered herself to her haunches, resting a hand on his thigh, warmth radiating from her.

His body reacted immediately. He tried to kill the urgent need he felt for her, reminding himself she was a monster, a killer, that she was using him.

"Using you?" she asked, tilting her head. "I would be annoyed that you're lying, but you're lying to yourself. It's human nature, I think." Her hand slid across his leg to his crotch, her deft fingers massaging his swiftly stiffening erection.

"Stop it," he hissed. "Stop it. My family is right there."

"Oh, is that your issue?" she asked, a mischievous smile crossing her pale, perfect face. The room around them grew darker. "They don't have to be. We can be alone." She leaned forward and planted a kiss against his lips. She was so soft, so perfect, so ...

NO! He tried to pull back, but his body didn't want to respond; it wanted her. He tried to think of his girlfriend, about anything other than how deftly her fingers moved across his body. Even through his jeans, he felt like he might lose control. The darkness swallowed them, leaving the entire world a void of emptiness other than Eli ... and her.

"What do you want with me?" he asked.

"Nothing you haven't given before," she responded, her fingers working free the button of his jeans. He reached down, trying to still her hands. She didn't stop what she was doing, but she looked up into his eyes as she slowly pulled his zipper down. "Nothing you don't want to give." She pushed aside the flap and wrapped her fingers around his erection, pulling it free from his jeans. She smiled at him. The smile was ... strangely sweet, inviting. The image of her as the bloody monster was deteriorating in his mind, leaving this willing, beautiful woman in its place.

"I can't ... I don't ..." he tried protesting, but she had reached behind his head with her other hand and was rolling back, pulling him forward and over her.

She wrapped her legs around his waist and, with her hand, guided him into her. He gasped as he felt the slight pop of entry. She felt so fantastically good. Otherworldly, not just inside her but against her too. Her body pressed against his as he started moving. He couldn't stop himself, as though he had no control over his actions. But he knew that was another lie he was telling himself. He didn't *want* to stop. He looked down at her as he thrust up, meeting her eyes. Her gaze was filled with so much promise; heaven and hell lurked there. Gehenna and Olam Haba'a, and everything between.

He lowered his head, pressing his lips to hers. For a moment, she stopped writhing under him, her lips stiff and resisting, and then she bucked against him, her tongue pushing past his lips, returning the kiss with a passion that overshadowed the act of fucking they were engaged in.

107

Wordlessly, they moved in unison in the darkness. He rose to his knees, his hands on her hips as he pushed her slip up so he could feel her skin on his. Soft, warm, inviting. He knew this was wrong, that he was damned for this. But he couldn't bring himself to stop. They fit together like machined parts that had been made specifically for each other. He only wanted to be with her, to please her, to be pleased by her. In his eyes, as in the shadowy void they were fucking in, there was only her, and him, and the sweat they shared.

He grunted, bending over as he worked to push deeper, feeling himself so close. The feeling of her body under his, her slender curves, and the movement of her muscles was too much. He wrapped his arms around her shoulders and pulled her tight as he slammed his hips into hers. She rose to meet his mouth again, her teeth tugging at his lips. He closed his eyes tightly as he felt himself explode in her, spending himself entirely. He collapsed on top of her, panting, feeling himself deflate and slowly slip out of her.

The horror of what she was, what she had done, seemed so distant to this moment. How could something so beautiful have happened with something so monstrous? It had to be impossible. And if it were all a fever dream or mold-induced insanity, then maybe none of this mattered. He looked at her, feeling his exhaustion catching up to him, as though the orgasm had been the only roadblock on his path towards sleep. He started to speak, to ask why these things were happening. But she lifted a hand and placed a single finger on his lips, silencing him. With that motion, the void closed in, and darkness took over all of creation.

11

Eli woke up with a start, feeling the cool air of a New York December morning brush across his penis. With a start, he realized his pants were down, but just as confusing, he was in his brother's bed again. When had he gotten up and changed rooms? He quickly looked himself over, searching for any blood he could find, but in the low light of the room, he just couldn't tell. He quickly pulled his pants up, tucked himself inside, and zipped them. He crept out of the room to the bathroom, flipping the switch and quietly cursing when the light didn't come on. He stepped out of the bathroom and headed for the living room, pausing as he saw a light move across the wall.

A moment later, his mother turned the corner and frowned as she saw him, a candle in her hand. "Elijah?" she asked.

"Yeah, Ima, it's me."

"When did you go to Dov's room?"

"I ... I don't know." That was the truth, although he assumed it had something to do with the intense dream. Dream? Maybe *vision* would be a better word for it if they were really tripping. The alternative was too awful, too surreal to even voice. "I think I just couldn't sleep, so I sort of zoned out and went to the bed. When did the power go out?"

She shook her head and shrugged but didn't question his motives for going to the bedroom. "Did you—?" she was about to ask something but stopped herself. "Have you seen Moshe?"

"Moshe?" he asked. "Was that one of the guys who ..." He stopped himself. Who else would she be talking about? Moses? "No, I haven't seen him. Is he not in the living room either?" he asked instead.

"Obviously not or I wouldn't be asking," she said dryly.

"Maybe he did what I did and found a bed to sleep on," Eli suggested.

Ruth made a disgusted face. The idea of a man who wasn't her husband sleeping in her or in Lilah's bed didn't sit well with her. But nonetheless, she started to move towards those rooms to check.

He followed after. He had to admit to himself that when he woke up, he was terrified he would be covered in blood, that there would be another dead man. But no one was screaming, and he found no evidence of foul play. There had been a fear that maybe, somehow, he *had* killed those two men while in the throes of his dream.

The other question he had to ask was: Why couldn't he resist the woman? Not in his dreams, not in whatever reality this was, whether it was visions or a stranger truth than he dared believe. He had been terrified of her last night, traumatized by what she had done to Schulman and to the two cops. But his desire for

111

her, his wanton need for her cut through all of that and left him gasping and grasping for her presence. Even now, when he pictured her, he wanted her. And he hated that. It made him feel weak, and the guilt he felt for cheating on Cynthia ... But was it cheating on her if it was a dream? Was it cheating on her if his attraction was supernatural? Yeah, it was, he decided. He wouldn't try to excuse someone's infidelity if they were drinking, and this couldn't be too different than that.

He just wanted to get out of here, get out of this. Eli followed his mother as she checked her bedroom, calling for Moshe, and then Lilah's room to repeat the process. "Where could he have gone?" Ruth wondered aloud as the two of them headed back into the living room.

"He wouldn't have left, would he?" Yitzak asked.

Everyone turned towards the foyer and the door.

"No ..." Erel said. "That wouldn't make any sense. It's pitch black out there."

"But he was talking about his wife. She was still in his apartment before ..." the third man—Eli recognized him as Joseph Turnowitz—said. Joseph had been living in the building for ages. He was the sort of fixture most people would find comforting, but Eli had always hated him for his bullshit *grampa to everyone* act that he tried to pull off while not really trying to actually be kind or having any wisdom to share.

"Surely, he would not try to get back there alone," Ruth

scoffed.

"What if the … what if that woman lured him away?" Lilah offered.

Everyone was silent at that thought.

"No. The most likely is that he went to try to find and protect his wife," Joseph said firmly. "He is a good man; he would not be tempted by the likes of that creature." The side-eye he showed Eli was not lost on anyone.

Eli felt his neck burn hot with shame. "Okay, look, we've been in here for a while. We should check. There's nothing saying that out there isn't normal. Maybe he woke up, checked for himself, and saw that he could get back to his apartment without any issue."

Yitzak nodded. "That makes sense." He rose from the couch and walked to the front door. "If everything is returned to normal, I'm going to go home. I'm sorry, Erel, but I can't be a party to what your sons have brought down upon us." He opened the door before Erel could respond to the blatant statement condemning both Eli and Dovev.

As light spilled out into the hallway, they were greeted by the grisly sight of Moshe crucified to the brick wall opposite their apartment. He had been stripped naked, nailed to the wall by his hands, elbows, and shoulders, and then sliced from the collar bone all the way down to his taint. It was all there, cast in excruciating plain detail. The two halves of his penis flopped to either side, still dripping with the gore his vivisection had entailed. His intestines sat in a pile on the ground before him. Eli thought he could see his liver, kidneys, and other organs in the slop. But most horrifying of all, he could see Moshe's lungs, and they were still inflating and deflating.

"He's alive," Eli croaked, hardly able believe what he was seeing.

"Moshe!" Yitzak cried, pushing past Eli to go to Moshe.

"Wait! Don't—" Eli shouted, trying to grab on to the man before he left the apartment, but he was too late.

As soon as Yitzak's foot hit the bricks outside the apartment, she was there. Her white dress was a blur, a white streak and flowing black ringlet hair trailing behind as she ripped Yitzak off the ground and dragged him screaming into the shadows. Eli gripped the door frame, partially in terror but partially to keep Joseph or Erel from running out of the room to try and help.

Neither man was dead yet, but Eli knew there wasn't a damn thing they could do for the crucified man; nothing would save him. His lungs were working, but that would stop. No force on Earth could keep him alive after what he had suffered. Yitzak's screams echoed through the maze-like hallways. He begged and pleaded for her to stop, screamed for help, and just plain screamed in terror and agony. All of his screams were accompanied by the sound of tearing flesh and the wet slaps of blood and meat against brick. The whole time, Eli stood there

114

in the door, acting as a bouncer to keep his father from running out to join him in death.

Finally, the sounds of struggling and terror subsided. The only noise was the quickened breathing of those in the apartment and the soft gurgles of Moshe's drawn-out death. Eli pushed back from the doorway and closed the door, relocking it. They stood in silence for a long moment, each dealing with the fear that gripped their throats, strangling the hope from them.

"You just stood there," Joseph finally said.

"There was nothing we could have done," Eli mumbled.

"Nothing? You didn't even try to save him, either of them! You come in here after leaving for so long, and you bring the malikim with you. How do we know you aren't in league with her?" The old man jammed his finger into Eli's chest.

Eli recoiled at the elderly man's touch, disgusted by him and his words. "You're a fucking idiot," he growled, surprised how quickly he fell into anger, but it felt good. This man jabbing his finger at him was something he could confront, something he wasn't afraid of. It felt so damn good to have even a sliver of power. "How would I be in cahoots with some demon woman? And remember, Joe, you all called me, you all asked *me* to come home. Not vice versa. I came because I was asked to come. None of this is my fault."

"The rebbe, he said she was latched on to you," Erel said

slowly.

"You too, Aba?" Eli asked, spinning on his dad. "You think I'm the one causing this? Think. Even if that is true, even if all of this isn't some fucking mind trip, wouldn't she have just latched onto someone else? Maybe she did before I came; maybe you were in bed dreaming of another woman while Mom lay there; maybe you just don't want to ad—"

Erel's fist crashed into his face, shutting him up.

It wasn't a terribly strong punch, but it shocked him. He had never seen his father so angry—in the past, he had always acted like physical punishment was a necessary evil of being a parent. Eli lifted a hand to his cheek, narrowing his eyes at his dad. Erel stood there shaking with rage, his hands balled into fists; it was almost comical. "So you can throw shitty accusations on anyone else, but if someone questions you, it's immediately justified to start hitting? I guess your pride is too important to swallow, huh?" The two men stared at each other for several tense moments.

"Erel, leave him alone." Ruth's voice cut through the tension like a dull knife through a firm tomato.

Erel's shoulders slowly fell as he released the tension, his fists uncurling as he turned away from Eli and walked to fall heavily onto the couch. Eli stood there, still feeling angry, ready to fight.

"And, Eli," Ruth continued. "Leave your father alone. These

are his friends, our neighbors, in a lot of ways, they are also our family. Just like you." She added that last part, and Eli felt himself deflate. He slunk to the couch and sat on the opposite end as his father.

"Sorry, Aba," he said, trying to keep some of the anger out of his voice.

"Me too, son. Me too. But don't ever bring your mother into your anger towards me. She deserves better," Erel said softly, neither man looking at the other.

"This is all fine and good, but it doesn't change the fact she is able to kill us because he is empowering her!" Joseph said, stepping up to the couch and crossing his arms over gut. "I say we give him to her, throw him in the hall. If he is gone, she will have no power!"

"Don't threaten my brother!" Lilah spat with a venom so sudden and malevolent that it startled everyone.

Joseph sputtered, taken aback to have Lilah, a young woman he had known since she was born, confronting him. "Not now, Lilah," he said dismissing her. "This is not the sort of thing you can understand; this is—"

"For men?" Lilah hissed.

"Yes," Joseph agreed, not hearing the dangerous tilt to her voice. "Grown men, not children or girls."

"Dude," Eli said, rubbing his eyes. "You sound like a fucking dinosaur."

117

"Lilah …" Erel said, shaking his head. "Respect your elders, and don't worry, Joseph is not going to do anything to Elijah. I promise."

"Don't be fast, Erel. I'm sorry it's your boy, I'm sorry it's your brother, Lilah, but my point stands. How many people are we going to let this monster kill while you protect the thing that enables her?" Joseph pressed.

"The rebbe never suggested we kill my brother!" Lilah nearly screamed.

"Well, the rebbe isn't here, and we don't have his knowledge or his skills!" Joseph shouted back.

"Hey, do not talk to my daughter that way!" Erel rose, joining the fray.

Within moments, everyone was shouting, filling the little apartment with noise. Joseph was getting more and more hysterical, more red in the face. Only Ruth stood to the side, not adding her voice to the typhoon of sound and anger that built in the room.

"You're just a miserable piece of shit who can't stand that he's in a situation he can't control!" Eli was shouting when Joseph stumbled back clutching at his chest. Eli was about to continue shouting, but as Joseph fell on his ass, gasping for breath, he faltered. "What … what's happening?" he asked, unsure what to do.

"Joseph!" Erel knelt next to the man, who was urgently

trying to get words out. Erel put his ear closer to Joseph's mouth. "His heart!" he suddenly exclaimed. "He needs his heart medication!"

Lilah ran to the couch where Joseph had thrown his coat, searching through the pockets while Eli watched, wide-eyed, as the elderly man sank lower on the floor. "Where is it?" she shouted. "I can't find it!"

"It must be back at his apartment!" Erel shouted back, and then realizing what he said, looked back at them with a significant look. Leaving the apartment was a death sentence. But leaving him without his meds was condemning Joseph to die. The four of them looked between each other, no one knowing what to do as they listened to Joseph struggling.

"Lilah, go to the restroom, get some aspirin!" Ruth suddenly spoke up, moving to push Erel out of the way and help Joseph lie down. "I ... he needs CPR until we can get help ..."

Lilah was running off to find the aspirin, while Erel and Eli stood there.

"Ima, there's no help coming. It's just us," Eli said softly.

Ruth ignored him, positioning herself over Joseph, putting her hands over his heart, and began pressing, counting each time to try to keep the rhythm. Eli listened to the sound of his mother's counting and Lilah rummaging in the dark for aspirin. It felt like he was back in the brick hallway, that each second was stretching outward towards eternity. He watched as Joseph went from red faced and panicked to the way his muscles relaxed. His body still shook as Ruth desperately performed CPR, but there was no other signs of life from him.

Lilah returned, running back to Ruth's side with the bottle, kneeling down as she reached them. Eli watched as Ruth continued to press on the dead man's chest, as Lilah tried to wake him so he could take the aspirin. One more death in this place, a drop in the ocean of loss that was drowning their entire world, and there wasn't a goddamned thing they could do about it.

12

The four of them sat in the living room, a sheet from the couch covering the corpse of Joseph. The air was suffocatingly thick with tension. Each member of the Rosenbaum family sat with their own thoughts, each unaware of how they could possibly rationalize all that had happened in the last four days.

"Elijah." Erel suddenly broke the silence. "Why did you come back?"

Eli looked up from the patch of floor he had been staring at for god knows how long. "What? You called me. Because of Dovev."

"Yes, I know that, but what made you decide to actually come? Why did you answer? Why are you here?" Erel pressed.

"Erel, what does it matter?" Ruth asked.

"It doesn't. I just want to know," Erel admitted. "You didn't plan on coming back. The fact that we were able to find your phone number, it wasn't easy. What if we couldn't get a hold of you? What if I or your mother had passed and no one reached out? Would you have come then? Would you have cared? Did you ever think about us? I just … I just want to know what brought you here."

"I don't know," Eli said, speaking honestly. He just didn't

see the point in pretending otherwise now. "I thought about it, about not coming, I mean. I was already at the airport, heading back home. But—"

"But what?" Lilah asked.

"I guess I felt like ... I felt like one day maybe I would see Dovev and Lilah again, that maybe once everything was said and done, they would do what I did and leave." He glanced up, knowing before he did that he would see the hurt on his mother and father's faces. He was less prepared to see the look of disgust on Lilah's. "Knowing that Dov was gone and that I was in town anyway, I felt like I didn't have a real choice. I missed Dov. I hated leaving him and Lilah here. But I knew I wouldn't have the resources to take care of them. I couldn't get them an education, couldn't feed them, none of that shit. How does an eighteen-year-old take care of themselves, let alone two younger kids?"

"You wanted to take them with you?" Erel asked, a sneer on his lips at the idea of someone taking his children from him.

"How did you take care of yourself?" Ruth asked, cutting off the dangerous line of questions from Erel.

"It was ... it was hard. I stayed with some secular friends until their parents got suspicious. I took the train south. Shaved my head. I worked weird jobs, and when I saved up enough, I signed up for a coding bootcamp, did enough little side gigs from library computers that I was able to actually get a pretty decent job. It was …" He suddenly laughed. "It was because of yeshivah I was way better at studying and memorization than any of the goyim I took classes with. It just came naturally to me. So I moved out to California, joined a software company. I've been there for about four years now. I live with my girlfriend."

"You live with her? You aren't married?" his mom asked.

Eli held up his hand. "No ring, not yet. I've been looking, though."

"What is she like?" He could hear the desperation in his mother's voice—she desperately needed this connection—and he was surprised to find that her interest, her need, made him feel warm, it made him feel more comfortable. He wanted her approval.

"Uh, Cynthia is …" He trailed off. He was trying to picture her, but in his mind, he only saw *her*. The white slip, the black hair and dark eyes. The winsome body that had writhed against him just last night. He shook his head. "She's great; you would like her."

"I'm guessing she's not a nice Jewish girl," Lilah said with a sardonic smile.

Eli chuckled and shook his head. "No, but, still … she's sweet, really nice, a good person. Isn't that what matters?"

"It is," Erel said. "You should emulate her."

"Erel," Ruth chided.

123

Erel shrugged and rose to walk to the kitchen and light another candle. They fell back into silence. Eli's eyes fell back to the shrouded form of Joseph lying in the middle of the living room.

"We should drag him ..." Eli paused. "We should put him in the hall," he finished.

"Elijah!" Ruth reprimanded. "That is unkind."

"He's dead, Ima. I promise he doesn't care," Eli said, too tired to argue more than that. "What does it matter if the body is out there instead of in here with us?"

"Maybe he was right," Erel said softly. "You're my son, Elijah, but you are so ... you are so far removed from decency that you would suggest such a thing. What would that monster do to his body? It is our duty as Jews, as friends, as family, to watch over his body to make sure it can be interred respectfully and without harm."

"And I'm saying that it's superstitious bullshit. What's going to happen is it's going to start stinking, and then a bunch of flies and maggots and other gross shit is going to get in here, and we're all going to get sick. You believe in germs, right? You know you can sick from being around corpses?"

"That corpse is one of my oldest friends!" Erel snapped. "And what do you propose? Toss him outside? Let him fester and rot with Moshe? How many need to die before you accept that maybe it isn't just superstitious nonsense?"

"Then what, Aba? We just sit around waiting to get some sort of infection from being around his body?"

"We would starve before," Lilah whispered. "Before we could die of infection."

"Jesus, Lilah," Eli said, frowning.

"It's true, though, isn't it? If we're trapped here, we might get infected, but we'll starve first, or she'll come back and finish it all."

"I—it's just such a morbid statement," Eli said lamely.

"Okay, but is it wrong? You keep telling everyone to be rational, to be more like you, so tell me. Am I wrong in some way?" Lilah curled her legs up under her and lay her head on the armrest of the couch. "Tell me I'm wrong and that everything is going to be okay."

Eli looked down, unable to respond.

"You are wrong. Everything will be okay." Erel lit another candle and lifted it. "I'm going to go for help." He began moving towards the door.

"Aba!" Lilah shouted

"Erel!" Ruth shouted at the exact same time. "You will not go out there!"

"Ruth, beloved, I have to."

"Why do you have to?" she asked, her voice dripping with stern admonishment.

"They are our children, Ruth. They are in danger. What else

can I do?" he asked.

In that moment, Eli saw him in a different light. More than ever, he looked like a man who was defeated, like someone who had been born here, lived here, and knew he would die here having changed nothing in the world. For the first time, he wondered what his father's dreams had been, what he wanted to do before he had surrendered to the life he had lived.

Ruth's face crumpled, and she nodded. Moving to the hallway closet, she took out his jacket and handed it to him before reaching back in for her shawl.

"Ruth, no, you need to stay here with the children," Erel said softly.

Ruth smiled and shook her head. "Don't urge me to leave you or to turn back from you. Where you go, I will go, and where you stay, I will stay. Where you die, I will die, and there, I will be buried. May the Lord deal with me, be it ever so severely, if even death separates you and me." She lifted her hand to him.

He looked at it and then her face before nodding solemnly and taking it. "You are holy to me, Ruth Rosenbaum."

"And you to me," she responded.

Erel opened the door and turned to face his children, not knowing if he would see them again but seeing no other way forward. He opened his mouth to speak, but no words came out. Behind him, lit by the flickering light of his candle, the bloody body of Moshe could still be seen in the shadows of the hallway.

Ruth squeezed his hand three times. "Elijah, Lilah. We love you."

Eli wanted to object. He looked between them and Lilah, wishing someone would stop this but not knowing what words he could even say. His parents were killing themselves. But they were doing it together, for him and for her. He wanted to scream at them to sit back down, that if anyone here deserved to die, it was him. But in that moment, as when he had run away a decade ago, he couldn't bear to risk himself for them. He looked down, filled with a terrible shame.

He didn't look up as he heard their footsteps and then the door close behind them, leaving him and Lilah in the silence of a near-empty apartment with only a corpse as company. Eli wanted to believe they would make it, that they were good enough people, holy enough that a demon couldn't get to them. That they would traverse that awful hallway, find a door, and escape to the outside world. Maybe they could get help, maybe the police would come and arrest him, but at least Lilah and his parents would be okay.

A sonorous, beautiful laughter filled the room from somewhere outside, followed by a blood-curdling scream. Then a silence so deep that Eli could hear his heart breaking. The only thing that broke the terrible silence was the sound of Lilah's sobs.

Eli didn't know how long they sat there in the living room, the corpse of Joseph their only company. His phone had died hours ago, and with the power off, there were no clocks to tell him when it was. It could be the middle of the night, or three days could have passed for all he knew. For them, the entire universe was that apartment, for outside was death. Eli wondered if the other tenants, the ones who had not been outside when the woman had attacked the police, were still alive. But he doubted it. She was toying with them, picking them off one by one or in twos. He didn't know why she was doing it; he doubted there was even a reason. But what he did know was at least three people had suggested that it was his fault. That he was the one causing all of this because of his dreams, because this beautiful monster had somehow chosen him to siphon strength from.

Was that all this was? Was this horrible nightmare maze they were trapped in just a manifestation of her power stolen from him? If he wasn't here, if he couldn't be used, would Lilah be free? Could he save at least one person? He looked over at his sister, his last living connection to the world. She sat where she had been sitting since their parents left, unmoving, barely breathing, so lost in her grief it seemed impossible to move on. He realized in that moment that though he had failed her so spectacularly before, he now had a chance to make it up to her;

he had the obligation. He was a lost cause who had gone through life dead inside and filled with anger, but she could still go out into the world and do good. She could do Tikkun Olam, and maybe he could do the same by giving her that chance. He rose and moved to the kitchen, lighting another two candles. He lifted one and moved towards the bathroom. He saw that she had moved, just a little, so that she could watch him.

"I'm just ... going to the bathroom," he said.

She met his eyes, seeming to stare through him before lowering her head again. He watched her for a few moments, burning her into his memory, strengthening his resolve, and walked into the bathroom, closing the door behind him.

THURSDAY

13

Eli looked at the closed door as the water filled the bathtub. He wasn't sure what he was doing anymore. He didn't know how to continue. Everything he had thought he had known, everything he had believed was a lie. And now both worlds, the rational world he had run to and the religious world he had fled from, were in shambles. He set the candle down on the sink and stared into the mirror. How long ago had he stared in this mirror at his dead brother's face? Had it been Dov's dybbuk trying to warn him, or just another trick by the creature that had torn his entire world apart?

He couldn't answer that. He pulled on the mirror, opening the medicine cabinet, and looked around. He had hoped to find sleeping pills, or valium, anything that could help him do what he needed to do as painlessly as possible. But there was nothing like that anywhere. Instead, there was a small opened box of razors. His heart sank, and fear filled him like an icy basin in the pit of his gut. He pulled one of the razors out, knowing he didn't have a choice.

He peeled out of his clothes, sweat stained after the hours—or days—of wearing them, and slipped into the bathtub, wincing as the warm water hit his cold skin. He was surprised the hot water heater was working. He had expected the water to be ice cold. Maybe he had hoped the cold water would kill the pain of what he was about to do. He lay there in the tub, staring at the razor in his hand. His chest throbbed as he choked back sobs of fear and pain.

"Would you like help?" her voice, so beautiful and sexy, whispered across his ears. He looked up to see the woman in white sitting on the edge of the bathtub staring at him.

"I don't want to die like they did. I'm scared," he admitted.

"Of course you are," she said, reaching out to take the razor from him. She set it on the sink and then reached down to pull her slip up over her head.

Despite the frantic sex he had with this woman, this was the first time he had actually seen her body. It was breathtaking, and his sudden need for her made him so angry. How could he want her after everything she had done? How could he be horny when his parents had just died, as he was going to ...?

"It is your nature, and it is mine," she answered his unspoken question. She picked the razor back up and moved to the bathtub, gently stepping over the edge and straddling him.

"No," he whispered, trying to dredge up his willpower to resist her.

"No?" she asked, genuinely seeming to be surprised.

"No. Every time ... you kill ... I don't want you to kill my sister. I need it to stop." Eli understood how pathetic his voice sounded in that moment, whimpering and begging.

"Oh, Eli," she said, stroking his face with her free hand. "If I promise not to hurt her, will you give yourself to me?"

"You promise? How can I trust you?"

"I am a woman of my word, Eli," she responded. "And I promise."

Slowly, he nodded. He didn't know if he would have actually been able to resist her if she'd insisted. Even now, after everything, she was the only thing he cared about, the only thing he wanted, overshadowing and blocking out almost all other thoughts. He couldn't remember Cynthia's face, not anymore, but he couldn't let her hurt Lilah.

She reached down to grab his now erect penis and guided it to her.

"Wait," he said suddenly, placing his hands on her waist.

She paused, meeting his eyes with an arched eyebrow.

"I don't even know your name."

She shook her head as if amused. "Do you want to?"

"Yes."

"I am called Pizna; you can call me Pizna." The name seemed to sit oddly on her lips, as though she was so unused to her name being used as for it to be alien. "Is there anything else,

Eli?"

He shook his head, and she lowered herself onto him. He gasped for air as he felt her surround him, her muscles squeezing him. She was as close to perfection as he had ever known. It felt as though he was made for being intimate with her, that she had been made for making love to him. She reached down and pulled his right hand away from her waist, carefully digging into the flesh of his wrist, cutting a deep line from his wrist towards his elbow. He felt his hand go numb, losing control of his fingers as she sliced through tendons. She dropped the hand and repeated the process on his left arm. She let his left hand fall and then reached down to tightly grip both forearms.

"What are you doing?" he asked as she began to move her hips, grinding against him

"Not before we're done. You owe me one more. I owe you one more. One more time together," she promised.

He closed his eyes, squeezing the tears out as they rocked together in the reddening water. It sloshed around them and spilled over the sides of the tub. His pain was evaporating. He could feel the cold spreading through him. Despite the growing numbness, he could still feel her body against him. The light flickering across her subtle curves and dancing on the walls made everything feel even more surreal, more dreamlike. He felt his body screaming for help but also screaming for release.

He could feel himself getting close. He tried to sit up so he could kiss her. If he were to die during this, he wanted to die with the taste of her on his lips.

She looked down at him and smiled, and it was surprisingly kind. She curled over him, meeting his lips with her softness, not pausing in her writhing. There, with their lips locked, she moaned as she came, the spasming and pulling of her vaginal muscles wringing an orgasm from him as she did. Spent, he relaxed, realizing he felt so, so sleepy.

She slowly released his arms, letting them sink into the blood-red water. She pulled herself off of him and stepped out of the bathtub to replace her slip.

"What day is it?" Eli asked, his eyes unfocused, staring at the moldering tile of the ceiling.

"Thursday," Pizna said gently.

"I'll never see another Shabbot. I wish I could light the candles one last time. I don't even know why, but I do," Eli whispered; he didn't have the strength for more.

"Would you like to say it?" Pizna asked. "The last words on a Jew's lips should be—"

"I don't think I can. I don't think I remember …"

"Would you like help?" she asked for the second time.

Weakly, Eli nodded.

"Shma, yisrael," Pizna started. Eli closed his eyes, mouthing the words with her, barely able to exhale anymore to voice them. He was spent, spiritually, physically, and emotionally. "Adonai eluheinu, Adonai echad."

His breathing was a ghost on his lips, his heart struggling to beat, as it had nothing to pump through empty veins.

"Baruch shem k'vod malchuto, l'olam va'ed," Pizna finished for him.

The barest flicker of motion crossed Eli's lips, or maybe it was just the shadow from the candle on the sink.

Pizna stood next to the bloody bathtub in her soaking wet slip, staring down at the body of Eli, when she heard the door open and then close.

"He's dead, Lilah."

"You were supposed to avenge my brother, not take another."

"I know that, child," Pizna agreed.

"Why?"

"You can't be surprised." She turned her eyes from the corpse of her lover in the red water to Lilah. "You asked that all culpable in Dovev's death pay. You invoked the Lillim; you called on me. Did you think I would act in half measures, Lilah? Did you think that Pizna is one for forgiveness?"

"He didn't—"

"Don't lie to yourself, child," Pizna interrupted. "You blamed him leaving as much as you blamed anything or anyone

135

else. There is a proverb: a child that is not embraced by the village will burn it down to feel warmth. Instead, Dovev allowed his fire to consume him. But you, you are burning it all down. You lit the match, and I am but the flame you summoned to end it all."

"No! I never meant for you to hurt my family. You killed them! You killed my Aba, my Ima, my brother. You've killed so many … for what? Because I was angry? You don't care about me any more than you cared about him!" She gestured to the serenely peaceful body of her brother.

"No, I don't care about you at all. Him, him I liked. I tried to take his pain away in the end. He was always going to die here, in this appointed place, at this appointed time. I did what I could to make it … pleasant." She sat on the edge of the tub and reached down to caress Eli's cold cheek. "Do you know what happens now?"

"Now that you've killed everyone?" Lilah spat.

"Yes. Now that everyone is dead, except you."

Lilah jerked her head towards Pizna, her eyes wide. She stepped away at the implied threat, her hand reaching for the door.

Pizna rose and stepped forward in one smooth motion, gently grabbing Lilah's arm and pulling it back. Her other hand reached up and pushed Lilah's hair out of her face. "I'm not going to hurt you, Lilah. What happens now is you carry this with you for the rest of your life. They killed your brother; you killed them." Pizna's eyes, as dark and deep as the starry night, searched Lilah's for several minutes.

"I don't know how," Lilah finally stuttered. "I don't think I can."

"No?" Pizna asked.

Lilah shook her head.

"No. I suppose not. Strong enough for rage but too weak for regret. How human." She reached behind her neck and pulled something from within her mane of black hair. "If you do not think you can countenance what I've done, what *we* have done, then don't." She pulled Lilah's hand up and placed something there, gently forcing Lilah's fingers closed around it. There was no kindness in her eyes, no gentleness in her words. She stepped past the girl and walked through the bathroom door into the gloom beyond, leaving Lilah standing alone with the dead.

Lilah opened her hand. There, she found the molar she had pulled out less than a week ago and a single bloodstained razor.

Made in United States
Orlando, FL
15 May 2025

61291189R00079